MYSTERY

Shawn Pierce

Copyright © 2015 Shawn Pierce
All rights reserved
First Edition

PAGE PUBLISHING, INC.
New York, NY

First originally published by Page Publishing, Inc. 2015

ISBN 978-1-68139-666-8 (pbk)
ISBN 978-1-68139-667-5 (digital)

Printed in the United States of America

Part 1

EPISODE 1

May 28, 2014

Today was Sean's birthday. As he sat in his apartment, thinking about how blessed he was to see another year, he gave thanks to the Lord. All of a sudden, his cell phone began to vibrate, letting him know that he had received a text message. The text message said, "Happy Birthday." Even though he didn't recognize the number, he texted back, "Thank you. Who is this?"

The mysterious person responded, "I have been watching you for a minute and wanted to say happy birthday. I'm at the Olive Garden right down the street and would love to meet you."

Sean was very surprised by this. He texted back, "Okay, I don't have any plans for the rest of the evening anyways. I am on my way."

So he got ready and went to meet this mysterious person. Sean only went because it was something to do for his birthday, and it was a public place. He hadn't done anything for his birthday, but stayed in the house watching movies. He didn't know many people here in Atlanta, and the ones he did know he wasn't close with for personal reasons.

Sean got to the restaurant and went in. The waitress greeted him at the door and showed him to the bar.

Waitress: Are you Sean?

He replied very slowly, "Yessss," wondering how she knew his name. Then, she went to the kitchen. Five minutes later, she came back with a drink, a slice of cake, and a note.

Waitress: This is for you. I was told to deliver this note to you when you got here.

Sean: Thank you.

The note read, "Happy Birthday. The drink and cake is on me. Enjoy then go back to your car."

Sean was now thinking he must be on bloopers or something. He played along and finished the cake and drink, and then left. As he approached his car, he saw a rose and another note on the windshield.

He said, "What the hell," and grinned at the same time in disbelief.

Find out what the note says on the next episode.

EPISODE 2

Sean took the note and rose, got in the car, and locked the doors. He opened the note and it read, "Happy Birthday again. I hope you enjoyed the cake and drink and liked the rose. A little about me, I am a thirty-eight-year-old Puerto Rican who owns a private investigation firm here in Atlanta. I wanted to join you but was kind of nervous. I really would like to meet you and to ease your mind. You can see me on your way home. You have to pass by my place to get to your place. I will be the redbone Puerto Rican you will see standing out."

So Sean was heading home, and when he turned into his community, he started looking like Peeping Tom. He passed by two places, nothing. Now he was driving up the hill and by another place. Still nothing. As he topped the hill to come down, he started seeing people in front of this one place. As he got closer and closer, he was driving like Miss Daisy at this point, but his doors are still locked. Then out of nowhere, he spotted, yep, a redbone Latino and so good looking. As soon as Sean drove by and waved at the Puerto Rican, his cell phone started ringing. It was them. He picked up and said, "Hello."

Then the conversation started. Sean was very surprised how the conversation and night went from here, but he enjoyed it.

*****Find out how the conversation goes and the night turns out on the next episode.*****

EPISODE 3

Sean: Hello.

Mystery person: Hello, how are you?

Sean: I am good, and you?

Mystery person: The same. I hope I didn't offend you by what I did today.

Sean: No, I wasn't offended. I was just surprised and shocked. I have never had anybody to do something like that for me before.

Mystery person: Oh, okay. Maybe I will get the chance to do something like that again for you.

Sean (smiling): You don't even know me.

Mystery person: I know that, but I will like to get to know you. Can that happen?

Sean: Why me?

Mystery person: Remember I told you that I have been checking you out for a while now? You seem like a nice and genuine person, and I need some positivity in my life. I've been divorced for a year now and finally ready to mingle again.

Sean (laughing out loud): I heard that. You know I have a thing for redbone Puerto Ricans, right?

Mystery person: Oh you do, huh? So can I take you out for a dinner and a movie, for a real date? You don't have to worry about anything. I will take care of everything. All you have to do is bless me with your presence.

Sean: Sure, when?

Mystery person: Next weekend, because I work crazy hours, and I will be able to take off then.

Sean: I need to ask you, how did you get my number?

Mystery person: If I tell you, you may feel uneasy about it and be angry, and I don't want to jeopardize this. But I am going to tell you anyway and hope for the best.

You will not believe what was done to obtain Sean's cell number. Find out on the next episode.

EPISODE 4

Sean was on the phone with this mystery person determined to find out how his cell number was obtained.

Mystery person: I will tell you how I got your cell number. It may make you feel uneasy and angry. Just promise you will give me the benefit of the doubt and don't think I'm weird or a stalker.

Sean: I will try, just tell me.

Sean just said "I will try" just to find out how his number was obtained.

Mystery person: I followed you one day around the mall. This particular day, you were wearing a green and white Rocawear shirt, cargo shorts, and green and white Adidas sneakers.

Sean was like for real. He was described all the way down to his shoes. At this point, he didn't know whether to think this mystery person was crazy or very observant.

Mystery person: You went into Foot Locker, and I went in behind you. You never saw me. This was the perfect opportunity for me cause the store was packed and really busy. I saw you looking around for someone to help you. Being that I was pressed for time for an interview with my firm, I had to make something happen. I already had on dress attire, so I stepped to you and asked, "May I help you?" You said, "Do you work here?" I commented yes and that I was the regional manager of all the stores. You wanted to see a pair of gray Adidas, and I asked what size and do you have a customer account here. When you replied, "Yes, and a size 9," I was like "Okay, I need your house or cell number to pull up your account," then you gave me your cell number. I told you I would be right back. I took the shoe and went to one of the real employees and said they could put this shoe back because it didn't fit me. Then I left the store with your cell number.

At this point, Sean's mouth was on the floor because he remembered that day. He remembered waiting and waiting. They never returned with the shoe, so he went up to the cashier and told her he had been waiting for like twenty minutes for the regional manager to bring him a certain shoe. Can he get some help? The cashier apologized but stated there was no regional manager in the store. Sean had said, "You're sure? Because he just took the shoe and asked for my size and number to pull up my account here." The cashier called and asked the store manager. The store manager replied the same way and added that the regional manager was in Chicago for meetings anyway. Sean said okay and left because at this point he was feeling kind of uneasy.

Even though he was feeling uneasy, that was *not* what was bothering him the most. What was bothering him was that he got to replaying that day at the mall in his head, and he remembered the so-called regional manager and exactly what he looked like, a good-looking redbone Puerto Rican, but this was *not* the same Puerto Rican that Sean saw and waved at tonight outside on his way home from the restaurant.

So now he is back to square one. Who did he actually wave at tonight, thinking he was the mystery person that left the rose and note? And who is the real mystery person pretending to be the regional manager? And which one is he talking on the phone with right now?

Find out who's who on the next episode.

EPISODE 5

As Sean and the mystery person continued the conversation, he began to wonder about a lot of things, so he started asking all kinds of questions.

Sean: Why would you go through all this trouble just to get my number?

Mystery person: I told you I had been watching you and wanted to get to know you. I just didn't know how you would respond to me, so I decided to go about it that way. I don't take rejection face to face really well.

Sean: I understand that, but the way you went about it would make people think you are crazy or a stalker, no pun intended.

Mystery person: Well, what do you think about me?

Sean: I can't say really.

Mystery person: Ask me anything. I have nothing to hide.

Sean: Okay, exactly how long have you been watching me? You said you have been divorced for a year now. What happened with that?

Mystery person: I have been watching you for about a month now. The first time we saw each other was in the business office of our community. You really didn't pay me any attention though. As for my divorce, it was a mutual understanding that we would be better off just friends.

Sean: Our community? So you live in the same community as me too? Oh, and I am sorry about your divorce.

Mystery person: Thanks, and yes, I do. When I am not at work, I see you when you leave, and I see you when you return. I even saw you when you came back from the restaurant tonight.

Sean: Speaking of that, I waved at someone tonight. I thought it was you.

Mystery person (laughing): Yeah, I saw that too, but it wasn't me.

Sean (laughing): That's not funny.

Mystery person: I tell you what. Walk outside on your balcony.

Sean: For what?

Mystery person: You want to see me, don't you? Just walk outside.

So Sean being curious put on his shoes and walked outside on the balcony. He was on the third floor, so he was looking toward the ground.

Mystery person: I see you.

Sean: Where are you? I don't see anybody down there.

Mystery person: I know because I am not down there. Look straight across from your balcony.

Sean looked straight across to another apartment building.

Sean: Are you serious? You live right across the way on the third floor?

Mystery person (laughing): Yep, I see a lot from here especially with my binoculars.

Sean: I bet, but it is dark, so I can't see you clearly. Looks like I am going to have to keep my blinds closed now.

Sean was so serious about that. It ain't no telling how long this has been going on.

Sean: Well, I need to go. I have to get up early for work.

Mystery person: No, don't go just yet. Can I come over for a little bit?

Sean: No, thanks.

Mystery person (laughing): Well, I am coming over anyway.

Sean: I said no, so have a good night.

He hung up the phone. Tonight has been really crazy, so he decided to get ready for bed. It hadn't been ten minutes since he hung up the phone with this mystery person. There was a knock on his door. He said, "What the hell? Now I know he ain't just show up at my door like this. That would be a total stalker move."

So Sean got his "loaded piece" and headed to the door. When he opened the door, he couldn't believe who was on the other side. It was the redbone Puerto Rican he waved at earlier tonight, the one he thought was the mystery person from the start. Sean was totally stunned.

You will never guess how this night plays out. Find out on the next episode.

EPISODE 6

Sean opened the door, and the person standing outside was the one he waved at earlier tonight. The one he thought was the mystery person. Now he is wondering, *What is this? Are people going crazy tonight?*

The conversation went as follows:

Sean: Yes?

Unknown person: What's up? Sorry to bother you, but I assumed you would want this.

As Sean began to say "Want what," he was presented with his wallet.

Sean: How did you get my wallet?

Unknown Person: I found it on the ground outside, so you had to drop it. I did look in it to see who it belonged to, and that's it. I just wanted to return it. Will you please check it out and make sure everything is there. It will make me feel better.

Sean: Sure.

As Sean checked the wallet out, to his surprise, everything was there, even down to the last dollar.

Sean: Thank you so much. I really appreciate you bringing it to me. Would you like to come in for a drink?

Unknown person: Sure, thanks, and no problem.

Sean: I have a bud light. Is that good?

He nodded yes.

Sean: You know you don't find too many good people these days that would have done what you did with the wallet.

Unknown person: I know right. I saw you waving at me tonight.

Sean: Yeah, I know. I thought you were someone else, my bad.

Unknown person (smiling): Umm, hmm, is that right.

Sean (smiling): What's that supposed to mean?

Unknown person: Nothing.

Sean: Is there anything I can do to show my appreciation for you bringing my wallet back? I could have been really messed up.

Unknown person: Yes, you could have, and yes, you can.

Sean thought to himself, Oh Lord, why I offered that. Guess they will ask to borrow money since I am sure they know it was $500 in the wallet.

Unknown person: Go out with me.

Sean: Excuse me. What do you mean go out with you?

Unknown person: Go out with me. I haven't had a friend to go out with in a long time. We can go to a bar and get a drink, catch a movie, just hang out. That's how you can repay me. On top of that, everything is on me.

Sean really couldn't say no 'cause after all that went down with his wallet. So he said, "Okay, what the hell. When?"

Unknown person: Tomorrow night. Here is my cell number. Text or call me tomorrow.

Sean: Okay, I'm Sean, by the way. What is your name?

Unknown person: Call me Mystery.

Mystery?

As he headed out the door, he gave this grin and said good night. As Sean closed the door, he said to himself, "This has been one crazy night."

If you think this night was crazy, wait until you hear about the next night with Mystery and the actual mystery person on the next episode.

EPISODE 7

Last night was indeed crazy. Sean is getting ready to go out with Mystery. They're just going to go to a bar and get a drink. It's the least he could do for what Mystery did for him with the wallet situation.

    Sean's cell phone rang.
    Sean: Hello.
    Mystery: You ready?
    Sean: Just about.
    Mystery: Okay, I'm on my way over.
    Sean: Okay, cool.
    They hung up. Sean's cell phone rings right back again.
    Sean: Yes, Mystery?
    Mystery person: And who is Mystery?
    Sean: Oh, I thought you were someone else.
    Mystery person: Obviously. So where are you going all dressed up?
    Sean: Are you serious? You really be looking into my place, don't you. I'm going to have to keep my blinds closed seriously.
    There was a knock at the door. Sean yelled out, "Come in," and Mystery stepped in.
    Sean: Okay, I have to go.

Mystery person: So you going to leave me hanging like that? Okay, I will see you out tonight.

Sean: Yeah.

He hung up.

So Sean and Mystery were at this bar downtown, drinking and talking when all of a sudden, Mystery's cell phone rings. After his conversation, Mystery says, "Will you excuse me for a minute?" Sean thought to himself, *Now I ain't no fool. Something is up.*

So he waited for about five minutes and got up to go outside. What did he see when he stepped outside? Mystery was kissing someone else. Sean was like, "Wow, really!" As he approached, they stopped, and Mystery looked up at him. All Sean said was "Handle your business" and walked back inside. As he was walking back inside, he could overhear Mystery say, "Who was that?"

He went back to the bar. Minutes later, Mystery comes back. Mystery could see something was bothering Sean.

Mystery: What's up? You okay? You seem agitated.

This conversation gets heated and shocking, but you will never guess how it turns out. Find out on the next episode.

EPISODE 8

Mystery: What's up? You okay? You seem agitated.
Sean: Are you serious right now? You really going to act like I just didn't see you?
Mystery: See me. Doing what? I was in the bathroom.
Sean: Okay, can we go? I'm ready to go home.
Mystery: I mean okay, but I honestly don't know what you are talking about.
So they're heading home, and Sean didn't say a word. He couldn't believe a person can look you in your face and flat-out lie. As they pull up to where he stayed, Mystery started.
Mystery: Something obviously got you upset.
Sean: Let's get something straight. I am not upset about anything. I am frustrated how you can deliberately lie to my face. I thought we were trying to be friends. I don't need friends like you.
Mystery: *I don't know what the hell you are talking about!*
Sean: Bye.
Sean got out the car and headed upstairs to his place without looking back. Soon as he got in the house, his phone rang.
Sean: What?
Mystery person: So you had a bad night, huh?

MYSTERY

Sean hung up the phone and cut it off. He was already pissed and didn't have time for games. So he took a shower and got ready for bed. He forgot he needed to take the trash to the dumpster. It's something about throwing onions in your trash can. So he slipped on his slippers and headed to the dumpsters and what did he see on his way there? Mystery standing outside his complex talking to the one he was kissing tonight. Sean was going to make himself seen this time, so Mystery couldn't lie.

Sean: Hey Mystery. How are you?

Then, he walked back to his place, cut his cell back on, and it rang.

With an attitude, Sean answered, "Hello."

Mystery: What is up?

Sean: You really going to call me with your kissing buddy right there. Can't lie now, can you friend? You could have spoken back though.

Mystery: There you go. What is it with you? I was calling to let you know . . .

As Sean got back to his door, Mystery was waiting outside on the phone with him. At this point, he was totally shocked.

Sean: How can you be here? I just saw you downstairs talking with your friend.

Mystery: No, you didn't. I have been standing here for the last five minutes.

Sean: Couldn't be. Do you have a twin or something?

Mystery: No, I'm the only child.

Sean: All jokes aside, you are the only child?

Mystery: Yes, why?

Sean: I believe you have a twin. I just saw someone that looks exactly like you.

The phone rang.

Sean: One second, Mystery. Hello.

Mystery person: Thanks for speaking to me a few minutes ago.

Sean (to himself): Oh my god, I can't believe this.

He finally saw who the mystery person was. He has the same face as Mystery. It was the mystery person he saw tonight kissing the stranger, not Mystery. The only thing was Mystery didn't know it. He has to have a twin.

Sean: Can I call you back?

Mystery person: Sure.

He hung up. He needed to tell Mystery everything, everything from the mystery person to the mystery person being his actual twin that he knows nothing about.

Sean: Come in. I need to tell you something.

Find out on the next episode how Mystery takes the news, especially when he finds out that this look-alike is Sean's mystery person.

EPISODE 9

Sean needed to tell Mystery everything, everything from the mystery person to the mystery person being his actual twin that he knows nothing about.

Sean: Come in. I need to tell you something.

Mystery: Tell me what? It sounds serious.

Sean: It is. Have a seat.

Mystery (very slowly): Okay. You got me kind of nervous.

Sean: I don't know how to start this off. Well, first off, you told me you are the only child, right?

Mystery: Yep, why.

Sean: Okay. A couple of days ago, it was my birthday.

Mystery: Well, happy belated birthday.

Sean: Thank you, but please let me finish.

Mystery (raising his hands): Okay.

Sean: I received a text from a mystery person saying happy birthday and to meet him at a restaurant. I don't normally do this, but I went. He never showed. He just left me a letter and a rose.

Mystery: What is this got to do with me?

Sean: Please, I am getting to it. That night was the same night you found my wallet, remember?

He nodded yes.

Sean: When we went out tonight, I saw this guy that look exactly like you kissing someone outside the bar. I just saw this same guy a few minutes ago outside the complex talking. I am telling you, all jokes aside, you two look exactly alike.

Mystery: Okay, so he has been calling you. Are you two a couple or something?

Sean: Oh no, nothing like that. It's just conversation. I have never met him.

Mystery: Well, I need to see this dude. Can you make that happen?

Sean: I believe I can. When?

Mystery: Tonight, right now.

Sean: Are you serious?

Mystery: Yes, call him. I would like to meet this person that looks so much like me.

Sean: Okay, hold on.

So Sean called the mystery person, and the conversation went as follows:

Mystery person: Hello, sweetness.

Sean: Are you still with your kissy friend?

Mystery person: No, and that's all they are, a kissy friend. So what's up with you?

Sean: Can you come by my place? I want to see you.

Mystery person: Oh, do you? Sure, I am walking over now.

Sean: Okay.

Sean hung up. He told Mystery to wait in the bathroom and do not come out until he tell him to.

About ten minutes later, there was a knock at the door. He went and opened the door. Sean was mesmerized by how much Mystery and the mystery person looked alike.

Sean: Hi.

Mystery person: And how are you, cutie?

Sean: I'm okay. How are you?

Mystery person: I am good now that you called.

Sean: Okay, look, before you say anything else, I have somebody here I want you to meet.

MYSTERY

Mystery person: Oh so you setting me up or something?

Sean: No.

Mystery person (laughing out loud): So you like group play?

Sean: No, absolutely not.

Mystery person: Okay, so where are they?

Sean: Mystery, you can come out.

Find out on the next episode what happens when these two meet. All kind of surprising information comes out.

EPISODE 10

Mystery person: Okay, so where are they?

Sean: Mystery, you can come out now.

As Sean said that, he watched the mystery person cross his arms. So he yelled out.

Sean: No, wait, Mystery.

He told the mystery person he would be right back. He went to the bathroom where Mystery was waiting.

Sean: Hey, you have to promise me something before you come out.

Mystery: What is that?

Sean: That when you see him, you will not get violent or anything. I don't want anything like that to go on when I am the one that set this up.

Mystery: Look I just want to meet him.

Sean (yelling): Promise me, if you want to continue being friends afterwards, you need to promise me.

Mystery: Alright. Okay, I promise. I promise to not get physical or violent.

Sean: Ok stay right here for a minute.

Mystery: Look, you need to hurry up. I am not going to stay in here much longer.

Sean went back to the living room.

Mystery person: So they don't want to meet me or what?

Sean: Mystery, you can come now.

As Mystery walked into the living room, his eyes and the mystery person's eyes locked. Silence fell. Sean watched Mystery as he looked in shocked.

Mystery: I can't believe this. It's like looking in the mirror.

Sean: I tried to tell you.

Sean turned to look at the mystery person. He had this arrogant smirk on his face. It really confused him.

Mystery: Who are you?

Mystery person: I am Brazil, your twin. We finally get to meet.

On the next episode, find out how Mystery reacts to the news of having a twin brother that he never knew about.

EPISODE 11

Mystery: Who are you?
    Brazil: I am Brazil, your twin. We finally get to meet.
    Mystery and Sean were both surprised by that comment.
    Mystery: What did you say?
    Brazil: I said my name is Brazil.
    Mystery cut him off.
    Mystery: No, I'm not talking about that. You said we finally get to meet like you already know me or something.
    Brazil: But I do.
    Mystery: You don't know me.
    Brazil: Oh, but I do. I know we were born in New Jersey. I know that we are both twenty-five years old and our birthday is the twenty-eighth of March.
    Sean could see Mystery getting angry and frustrated.
    Mystery: I don't care what you think you know about me. You are not my brother.
    Brazil: Tell me, is everything I just told you true?
    Mystery: Yes, so what? I mean, what you do, research me or something? Are you some kind of stalker or something?

Brazil: No, I am not. I have been following you for years now, Mystery. When I found out I had a twin brother, I had to find you.

Mystery: And how did you find out?

Brazil: Our mother . . .

Mystery (interrupting): Your mother.

Brazil: Our mother told me when I turned eighteen. She also told me the story behind the reason she gave you up and kept me, but that is a story for her to tell you, not me. She just made me promise to stay away from you, but I couldn't.

Mystery: I don't need to hear anything from your mother. I need to talk to mine.

Brazil: When you do, ask her about the twin boy she took from the hospital.

Mystery looked like he could go through Brazil. He turned to Sean and said, "I got to go. I will talk to you later." He nodded yes. As he headed to the door and walked by Brazil, he bumped him and closed the door. Brazil just laughed.

Sean: What is so funny? I don't see anything funny about this situation.

Brazil: Remember, you are the one that brought us together. I just didn't think this would be the way I would meet him.

Sean: It's getting late, and I can't process anymore of this tonight. I need you to leave.

Brazil: So are you throwing me out?

Sean: That is you if you take it that way. I just need to be alone right now. So you have good night.

Brazil: Okay, I will call and check on you tomorrow.

He left, and Sean laid across his sofa. He would not be going to sleep no time soon for sure.

Meanwhile, as Mystery approached his house, he debated on how to handle this with his mother. He was really upset and was hoping it was not true. He walked in.

Mystery: Mom?

Gloria: I'm in the kitchen babe.

Mystery walked slowly in the kitchen. Gloria was a sixty-year-old woman standing only 5'5" to his 6'2". She always wore her hair in a ball.

Gloria: Hey baby, I made your favorite, chicken and rice.
She saw something was on his mind.
Gloria: What's wrong?
Mystery: I need to ask you something.
Gloria: Okay, go ahead.
Mystery: I just met this guy. He said his name is Brazil and that he has been knowing me for years.
Gloria: Okay, is he nice?
Mystery: He is my twin.
Gloria had to catch her breath.
Gloria: What. You don't have a twin. You are the only child I have.
She was talking really nervous now.
Mystery: Mom, this guy looks identical to me, a splitting image. Now I am going to ask you this. I have never known you to lie to me. Are you my real mother?
Gloria thought this day would never come. She thought she had covered everything from him. She answered slowly, "In every sense of the word, yes, I am your mother, but I am not your biological mother."
Mystery: Oh my god, he was telling the truth. How could you keep something like this from me? Then I had to find out from somebody else.
Gloria: I didn't want you to ever find out.
Mystery: Are you serious? You were never going to tell me? How could you?
Both their voices began to raise.
Gloria: If you knew the reason why, you would be grateful. You should be grateful. Haven't I given you any and everything you wanted growing up? I work two jobs to make sure you had.
Mystery: I have a twin brother I just found out about. Did you steal me from the hospital? He told me to ask about the twin boy you took from the hospital.
Gloria: Took you, yes. Steal you, no. You don't know what happened back then.
Mystery: If you would do something like that, you are no better than the woman that had me.

She slapped him before she knew. Silence fell as she covered her mouth with her hands. Mystery stared at her and said, "You are no mother of mine" and walked away.

Gloria called out to him, "Mystery? Baby?" The only thing she could hear was the door slammed. She began to breathe really fast. She reached for her blood pressure pills. As she did, a sharp pain went up her left arm. She grabbed herself. She tried to open the pill bottle but couldn't for all the shaking. The pain grew. She now could feel her chest tightening with every breath she took. She never felt pain like this before. "Mystery," she called out barely, and then, she hit the floor, gasping for air like a fish out of water, as her eyes closed.

Mystery found his way back to Sean's door. He knocked.

Sean: Coming.

As Sean opened the door, he could see Mystery standing there, and it looked like he had been crying.

Mystery: I didn't know where else to go.

Sean: Come on in.

On the season finale, true feelings are expressed, and another shocking secret is revealed.

EPISODE 12— SEASON FINALE

As Sean opened the door, Mystery was standing there, and it looked like he had been crying.

Mystery: I didn't know where else to go.

Sean: Come on in.

They both sat on the sofa.

Mystery: Sorry to come back. I know it's late.

Sean: Don't worry about it. I couldn't sleep anyways. How did it go with your mother?

Mystery: Not good. Not good at all. She admitted that it was true.

Sean: Oh wooooow. I'm sorry.

Mystery: She kept this from me all these years. And the worst part is that she wasn't even going to tell me.

Sean: Come on now, you don't know that.

Mystery (raising his voice): I do know. She admitted that too. She said she never wanted me to find out for some stupid reason.

Sean: What was the reason?

Mystery: I don't know. It didn't matter to me at the time. I didn't even want to hear it.

Sean: Sounds like you two really got into it.

Mystery: We did. I told her she was no better that the woman that gave birth to me, and then, she slapped me. Then I told her she was no mother of mine, and I left.

Sean: You were upset. You didn't mean that.

Mystery: Of course not. I was just angry. At the end of the day, I love my mom. It's just going to be hard to get past this.

Sean (rubbing Mystery on his back): It's going to be okay. You just need to sit down with your mom and listen to what she got to say.

Mystery: Yeah, I know.

Mystery looked up at Sean and just stared.

Sean: What?

Mystery: Nothing, I just like looking at you. You're a really sweet person.

Sean: Awwww, thanks. I try to be.

Mystery: You really are, and I like you for that.

Sean (smiling): Awwwww, I like you to.

Mystery: No, you don't understand. I really like you.

Mystery leaned over to kiss him, but Sean leaned back.

Sean: Come on, Mystery, what are you doing?

Mystery: What does it look like?

He leaned over again and Sean leaned back again.

Sean: It has been a long night, and you're upset. You have just found out that you have a twin brother, and your mother knew about it and has been keeping it from you all these years. That's a lot to process.

Mystery: True, but I don't want to think about that right now. I just told you I like you.

Sean: I know, but we are friends, Mystery.

Mystery: I know, but I would like to be more than that.

Sean stood up.

Sean: I'm flattered, but that can't happen. Trust me.

He stood up.

Mystery: Why, because of my twin brother?

Sean: No, he has nothing to do with it.

Mystery: Then why not? You don't feel anything for me? I know you do. I feel it every time we are around each other. Say it's not true.

Sean: Yes, I feel it, but nothing can come of it.

Mystery began to get frustrated.

Mystery: Why not? It's me isn't it? Just say it. It's because now you know I'm gay, and you feel some kind of way.

Sean: No, it's not you and definitely not that. I knew you were gay the first time we met. It's just me trust me. Look, Mystery, I like you. I like you a lot. I really do. You're a nice and caring person. I wish I could be with you, but we can't.

Mystery: Why you keep saying that? All you have to do is say yes.

Sean raised his voice, getting agitated.

Sean: I can't. Please stop asking me.

Now both of their voices are getting louder.

Mystery (grabbing Sean into his arms): No, I will not stop asking. You just said you wish you could be with me. What is holding you back? What is keeping you from making yourself happy?

Sean: Let it go.

Mystery: No tell me. What is it?

As Sean broke free from Mystery's gripping hug, he yelled, "*Because I'm a woman!* I'm a woman, I'm a woman." Tears started flowing.

Mystery: What did you say?

Sean: I'm a woman, Mystery.

Mystery: You don't have to go that far to reject me. I'm out of here.

As he turned to head for the door, Sean called out, "Mystery, wait." He stopped and, without turning around, said, "You have said enough for me."

Sean: Turn around and look at me.

Mystery: I'm good.

Sean (yelling): *Turn around!*

Mystery turned and looked at him.

Sean: Take a good look at me.

Sean reached and unbuckled his belt and took it off. He then unbuttoned his baggy shorts and unzipped them. They fell to the floor.

Mystery: What are you doing?

Sean didn't answer, just continued. As his shorts fell to the floor, his XL shirt fell just midway his thighs. Then he reached and slid down his boxers. It was dead silence. Sean took a deep breath and pulled up his shirt. The truth was there looking at Mystery in his face.

Sean watched Mystery, his mouth opened slightly in disbelief. His lips began to tremble, and his eyes began to gloss. He was devastated with what he was seeing.

"Oh my god. It's true," Mystery said in a low voice. As he said these words, Sean watched as a single tear scroll down the left side of Mystery's face.

Sean: My name is not Sean. It's Alexandria . . .

To be continued.

Part 2

EPISODE 1

Alexandria: My name is not Sean. It's Alexandria.

Mystery was so upset and shocked.

Mystery: How can this be? You have been pretending the whole time?

Alexandria pulled up her boxer and shorts and got herself together.

Alexandria: There is a reason behind all of this, Mystery. I never thought that you would actually fall for me, and I would have to do this.

Mystery: Don't say another word. You have been lying to me. I will not believe anything that comes out your mouth right now. I'm very humiliated and embarrassed. You accused me of lying to you when I wasn't. It was actually you who were lying the whole time.

Alexandria: Mystery, I'm sorry I hurt you, but I couldn't tell you.

Mystery: You are such a hypocrite.

Alexandria went to reach for him, and he yelled, "Don't come near me! As a matter of fact, you stay away from me. It's like you told me before, I don't need friends like you. I'm out."

Mystery walked out and slammed the door. Alexandria felt so bad, but she couldn't lead him on. That would have been really wrong. She would let him cool off and call him in a few days.

Mystery walked back to his house. It was around 11:00 p.m. at this point, and he knew his mother would have been in the bed by now. This he was sure and happy of because he didn't need another fight tonight with anyone. He just wanted to go to bed.

He made it home and went inside. He saw the kitchen light was on, but that wasn't anything unusual as they always left it on at night. He went upstairs and saw his mother's door closed, so he went on into his room and sat on the bed. A few minutes later, Mystery got up and took a shower and went to bed for the night.

On the next episode, Brazil gets an unexpected visitor.

EPISODE 2

As Alexandria woke up this morning, she turned over to look at the clock. It was almost twelve. She didn't realize that she had slept in that long. She guessed from everything that went down last night, her body was tired and drained. She sat up in the bed and just sat there, thinking about Mystery and how hurt he was to learn the truth. She would give him a call in a few days after she know he has had time to cool off and process everything about her. Even though they could not be together, she still liked and cared about Mystery as a friend.

The phone rang.

Alexandria: Hello.

Brazil: Hello, Sean. Did I wake you?

Alexandria: No, I am just getting up.

Brazil: I think we should talk. I would like to clear some things up with you. Can I come over, please?

Even though Brazil is very flirtatious and playful on the phone, Alexandria could tell from his voice that he was serious this time. So she said, "Sure, give me an hour and come on over."

Brazil: Okay, I will be over then.

So Alexandria got up and brushed her teeth, showered, and put some clothes on. She put some coffee on cause she had to have her caffeine in the morning. Then again, Mystery crossed my mind.

Mystery's House

Mystery just laid there in bed staring at the ceiling. He had learned so much last night and didn't know if he could trust anybody at this point. He, all of a sudden, realized that he didn't smell anything cooking. He was always awaken every morning with the aroma of his mother cooking some kind of breakfast. Mystery got up and went to his mother's door and knocked. "Mama, you awake?" No answer. "Mama, you in there?" Still no answer. He opened the door and saw that her bed was made up. He yelled downstairs, "Mama!" There was still no answer. Mystery headed downstairs and into the kitchen. There he found his mama on the floor, unconscious with her blood pressure pills all over the floor. "Mama!" he yelled out. "Mama, oh God, Mama!" He turned her over and saw she was not breathing. "No, no, no, Mama. Wake up, Mama. Wake up." He ran to his cell phone and called 911.

Operator: 911, what's your emergency?

Mystery (crying and yelling): I need an ambulance. My mama is not breathing.

Operator: Okay, calm down, sir. What is your address?

Mystery: 111 Crawford Street, Apartment 1010. Please hurry, she is not breathing.

Operator: I am sending an ambulance now to you. They should be there in ten minutes. Tell me what happed?

Mystery: I don't know. I came down stairs and found her on the floor.

Operator: Okay, the ambulance is on the way.

To Mystery, it seemed like an hour, plus the operator was asking all kinds of question. All of a sudden, he could hear the sirens. He ran to the door. The ambulance was pulling up. "She's in here!" Mystery called. The paramedics rushed in and began to work on Gloria, giving her CPR and oxygen. Mystery was about to go crazy.

Paramedic: I have a pulse. It is very weak though. We need to get her to Emory right now.

Mystery: I'm coming with you.

They loaded Gloria in the ambulance and took off.

Alexandria's Place

Alexandria could hear the sirens. She wondered what was going on now. There was not one weekend that goes by where she doesn't hear a police or ambulance. She fixed her coffee and sat down on the sofa to watch TV. Brazil will be over in a minute, and she couldn't wait to see what he actually has to say about everything.

Brazil's House

Brazil had finished getting dressed. As Brazil slipped on his shoes, there was a knock at his door. "I'm coming," Brazil said. Brazil was wondering who this could be because he doesn't get much company. There was another louder and harder knock this time. "I said I'm coming." When he opened the door, he couldn't believe who it was.

At the Hospital

The ambulance finally made it to the hospital. They rushed Gloria to the back as she had flat-lined on her way there. As Mystery was instructed to stay in the waiting room, he began to think about the last thing he said to his mother: "You are no mother of mine." This was weighing on him heavily because he didn't mean it. He had to tell his mama that, that he didn't mean it and that he love her. After about twenty minutes, the doctor came to the waiting room to speak with him. Mystery was crying and shaking. "How is she, Doctor? Is she going to be okay? Please tell me she is going to be okay."

> ***On the next episode, how will Mystery react to the devastating news about his mother and who is the unexpected visitor to see Brazil?***

EPISODE 3

Mystery: How is she, Doctor? Is she going to be okay? Please tell me she is going to be okay.

Doctor: Gloria, I mean your mom, suffered a major heart attack. When I examined her, it looked like she was unconscious and went without oxygen to the brain for a long time, which did more damage.

Tears continued to flow down Mystery's face. Over the last twenty-four hours, everything seemed to have turned against him.

Mystery: Is she alive?

Doctor: I'm sorry, but there is no brain activity. The only thing keeping her alive now are the machines. I'm so sorry.

Mystery: Can I see her?

Doctor: Sure, come with me.

The doctor showed Mystery to his mother's room. When Mystery saw all the machines hooked up to his mother, he just broke down. He could not stop the crying. He never cried so much in his life, but he didn't care because this was his mother. He wanted her to wake up.

Doctor: I will give you some time alone with her. I have a phone call to make and will be back to check on you both.

Mystery didn't say anything. He got in bed with his mom and laid his head on her stomach and wrapped his arm around her and just laid there in silence.

Brazil's Place

Brazil snatched the door open. "Yes?"

There was a woman and child standing there.

Ivy: Is that anyway to greet your ex-wife and mother of your child.

Brazil: Ivy?

Ivan: Daddy.

The child ran and jumped in Brazil's arms.

Brazil: Heeeey, lil man. I believe you have grown a few inches since the last time I saw you.

Ivy: Well, are you going to invite us in?

Brazil was stunned that they were here. "Come in."

Ivy was a petite lady the same age as Brazil. They were college sweethearts. Ivan was a seven-year-old who loved his dad. Even though they were not together, Brazil stayed in constant contact with them both and visited several times throughout the year.

Brazil: You could have told me you were coming.

Ivy: Well, if someone answered their phone or at least return a phone call, you would have known. Besides, your son wanted to see his dad, and I had the time to take off, so here we are.

Brazil: How long will you be staying?

Ivy: I don't know. A few days, I guess.

Ivan: Mama and I are going to move here.

Brazil: Oh, is that so?

Brazil glanced over at Ivy. Ivan was hugged up with his dad and so happy to see him.

Brazil: Hey, lil man, I got a new game for my Xbox. Go see if you can figure it out while I talk to your mom.

Ivan: Are you coming to play too?

Brazil: Be there shortly.

Ivan ran to the back bedroom.

Brazil: So what did he mean by that?

Ivy: You know how your son is. Always reading into things.

Brazil: Don't joke with me, Ivy. He just would not have mentioned that.

Ivy: I may have mentioned it on the phone with my dad. You know this is my hometown, right? I only moved to New Jersey to go to college. I think I need a change in scenery. You act like you don't want us here. What's up with that? I would think you would be thrilled to have your son nearby.

Brazil: Don't do that. You know I'm always happy to see Ivan.

Ivy: It's not set in stone anyway.

Ivan yelled from the back room, "Daddy, come on."

Brazil: I'm coming.

Ivy: I know I'm just getting here, but can you watch him until I get back? I want to go see my dad. This was the first stop we made when we left the airport.

Brazil: Sure.

Ivy left and Brazil headed to the back room to play the game with Ivan.

At the Hospital

Mystery was now sitting in the chair holding his mother's hand and just staring at her. The doctor knocked and came in.

Doctor: Come with me.

They walked over to an empty waiting room.

Doctor: There is still no sign of brain activity.

Mystery (interrupting): You basically saying my mama is brain dead.

Doctor: I'm sorry, but yes.

Mystery: So what I do now?

Doctor: That is strictly up to you. I would never tell someone to take a loved one off a machine that was keeping them alive. No matter what, there is still hope. At the end of the day, that is a decision you will need to make along with your aunt.

Mystery: Aunt? I don't have an aunt.

Doctor: You do. Your mom made it perfectly clear that if something like this happened, contact her next of kin, her sister. I have already given her a call, and she will be here this evening.

Mystery was wondering what else his mother had kept from him. He will need to have a long talk with her when she gets better, but for now, all he wanted is for her to wake up. "Thanks, Doctor."

Doctor: You don't remember me, do you?

On the next episode, we meet Gloria's sister and find out how the doctor knows Mystery.

EPISODE 4

Doctor: You don't remember me, do you?

Mystery: No, I don't. Sorry.

Doctor: I didn't think so. You were a little boy then. Your mom and I went to the same church years ago and became really good friends. Then she had to stop coming because she had gotten a second job, which interfered with service time. She was a good holy woman.

Mystery: Please don't talk about her in past tense.

Doctor: Sorry, you are right. She is a good holy woman. You had to be about six or seven then. You and my son used to play all over the church, couldn't keep you two apart.

Mystery: It seems like I remember something like that. What is your son's name?

Doctor: Clay.

Mystery: Oh, okay. How is he?

Doctor: I honestly don't know. We haven't talked in a long time, but that is a story for another time. I have some other patients to check on. I will stop by to check on Gloria before I leave today.

Alexandria's Place

The phone rang.

Alexandria: Hello.

Brazil: Hey, I haven't forgotten. I got some unexpected company.

Alexandria: No problem, I figured you would come up with something.

Brazil: No, I'm serious. My son is here right now.

Alexandria: Your son?

Brazil: Yes, but if you want, you can come over, and we can still talk. I just got through playing the game with him. I really would like to straighten everything between us.

Alexandria: Tell you what. I will cook dinner tomorrow night. If you are free, you can come over around eight, and we can go from there. Deal?

Brazil: That's a deal.

At the Hospital

Mystery was walking back to his mother's room. He had been outside smoking. When he got to the room, there was a woman in there.

Mystery: May I help you?

The lady looked stunned and surprise.

Diane: Hey, Mystery. I'm your Aunt Diane. You can call me Aunt Di.

She gave him a hug.

Diane was a middle-aged woman. She had been married twice and was sitting pretty from the divorce settlements from both. You can also see that she was or used to be some kind of addict.

Mystery: I'm sorry, but I didn't know my mom had a sister.

Diane: That doesn't surprise me. Your mom and I never got along.

Mystery: Why you say that?

Diane: Well, I'm fifteen years younger than your mom. Our parents died when I was only five, so Gloria had to raise me. I can say I did give her hell when I was growing up. We had a huge fight when I was barely in high school. Long story short, I dropped out and ran away. But anyway, enough of all that. The doctor told me her diagnosis, and I want you to know I am okay with whatever decision you make.

Mystery: I'm not ready to let her go.

Diane: Then don't, baby. Look, I need to go check into the hotel, so I will be back a little later.

Mystery: You don't have to stay at a hotel. Our house is big enough, and also, you are family.

Diane: Thank you, Mystery. I appreciate that, but I'm sure your mom wouldn't want me there if she was up and talking. I'm okay staying at the hotel.

Diane kissed her sister and left.

Brazil's Place

A few hours had passed, and Brazil had just finished cooking dinner for him and Ivan when there was a knock at the door.

Brazil: Coming. Be right back, Ivan. I think your mom has made it back.

When Brazil opened the door, he was shocked.

Brazil: Mom?

Diane: Hello, son.

On the next episode, Brazil and Diane have a serious conversation.

EPISODE 5

Brazil: Mom?

Diane: Hello, son.

Before Brazil could say anything else, Diane was walking on into his place.

Diane: Aren't you going to give me a hug?

Brazil gave his mom a hug and kiss.

Diane: I haven't seen you since you left for college. That was seven years ago.

Brazil: Mom, you know why I never came back home. I couldn't stand that guy you were married to, but that didn't matter to you. Anyway, I always called you and stayed in touch. You always knew where I was each time I moved.

Diane: Don't put it all off on Mark. Yes, you didn't like him, but after I told you about your twin brother, you just became obsessed with finding him after I continuously told you to let him be.

Brazil: It was hell growing up in that house with him. Two years, Mom, two years I dealt with it, and nothing mattered to you but him supplying you with your drugs, so excuse me for wanting to reach out to my brother and see if I could have some kind of real family relationship.

Diane: Don't get smart with me. I'm still your mother. Yes, I had a problem, but that is behind me now. Whatever hardship you had growing up, it paid off. Look at what you have. You are finally stable with a college degree and your PI license. I am very proud of you son.

Brazil: You know I should thank you. It is because of you that I went in the private investigation field. You told me about my brother but would never tell me where he was when you knew the whole time.

Diane: Yes, I did, but I didn't want you to get involved in his life, but that didn't stop you from finding him. It's amazing how much you two look alike.

Brazil: Have you seen him?

Diane: Yes.

At the Hospital

The doctor was in his office, looking over paperwork when there was a knock on his door.

Doctor: Come in.

Ivy: Hi, Dad.

Doctor: Baby girl.

They hugged each other, and the doctor kissed her on the cheek. They haven't seen each other in a few years.

Doctor: How have you been? Oh, I missed you so much.

Ivy: I've been doing well, and I miss you to. I just got in town a couple hours ago.

Doctor: Where is my grandson? I want to see him.

Ivy: You will. He is with father right now.

Doctor: His father?

Ivy: Yes, Dad, but we can talk about that later. How are Clay and Malik?

Doctor: Well, you know your brothers. I haven't talked to either one of them in a few weeks now. Maybe if they knew you were in town, they will come by the house and visit. You are staying with me at the house, right?

Ivy: Sure I am. I will give them both a call when I get to the house. Maybe we all can have dinner together tomorrow tonight.

Doctor: Good luck with that. You know your brothers don't get along.

Ivy: Maybe I can change that even if it is only for a few hours. Well, I just stopped by to let you know I was in town. I know you are busy, so I will let you get back to work. I am going to go pick up Ivan and be to the house when you get there.

Doctor: Okay, baby. Love you.

Ivy: Love you too.

Ivy left.

Brazil's Place

Brazil: You have seen him. What did you say to him?

Diane: He doesn't know who I am, and I will like to keep it that way. I saw him at the hospital when I was visiting a friend.

Brazil: Why was he there?

Diane: I think I overheard the doctor saying his mother had a heart attack.

Brazil: Oh, I'm sorry to hear that. Well, we both know who his real mother is, don't we, Mom.

Diane: Like I told you, I don't want him to know. He has a good life here without me or you getting involved.

Brazil was looking like he was guilty of something.

Diane: What is that look for? Have you spoken to him?

Brazil: Yes, but it's not how you think. A lady got tied up between us and brought us together. I didn't know she was going to do that.

Diane: Oh my god, Brazil. What does he know?

Brazil: He only knows that we are twins, nothing else. Furthermore, he doesn't care to know anything else. He made that perfectly clear.

Diane: I want you to stay away from him. You hear me?

Just when Brazil got ready to respond, Ivan came from the back.

Ivan: Dad, I don't feel well. My stomach hurts.

Diane was shocked.
Diane: Brazil, you have a son?

On the next episode, Diane meets her grandson for the first time. Brazil has more explaining to do.

EPISODE 6

Diane: Brazil, you have a son?

Brazil: Hey, lil man, come here.

Brazil picked him up and patted him on the back. "I will get you something for your stomach. I like you to meet someone. This is my mom, your grandmother."

Ivan: Hello.

Diane had tears in her eyes. She said, "Hey, little one, you look just like your dad."

Brazil: Okay, how about we go get something for your stomach.

They walked to the kitchen. Diane couldn't believe she was a grandmother.

Alexandria's Place

Alexandria hadn't made her daily call yet to her sister to check on how things were going, so she decided call her.

Adriana: Hello.

Alexandria: Hey, sis, how is everything?

Adriana: Hey, everything is good. We were just getting back from the store.

Alexandria: Let me talk to him for a minute.
Adriana: Okay, hold on.
Jase: Hello.
Alexandria: Hey, babe. It's Mom.
Jase: Mom, are you coming to get me?

Adriana was Alexandria's older sister who was looking after her son for a little while. She didn't mind at all as she couldn't have any kids of her own, and Jase was her only nephew. Jase was five and had never been away from Alexandria this long. It's been almost six months now.

Alexandria: I am coming to get you very soon, I promise. Let Mommy get everything perfect here first, okay? Are you having fun with Aunt Adriana and Uncle Max?
Jase: Yes, but I am ready to see you.
Alexandria: You will very soon. Let me talk to your auntie for a minute. I love you.
Jase: Love you too. Aunt Adriana?
Adriana came back to the phone.
Alexandria: I hate that he can't be with me right now.
Adriana: Don't worry about it. He can stay as long as you need him to. Is everything okay with you? Have you heard anything?
Alexandria: No, which is a good thing. I'm going to give it another month, and if everything is okay, I will be there to pick up Jase.
Adriana: Okay, you take care. Love you.
Alexandria: Love you too, and I will call tomorrow.

They hung up. All Alexandria could do was pray that this next month go by smoothly so she can go get her son.

Brazil's Place

Brazil came from the bedroom. He had given Ivan some medicine and laid him down.

Diane: Brazil, why didn't you tell me I had a grandson?
Brazil: Ivy and I chose not to. We didn't want him associated with you while you were still with Mark and doing drugs.

Diane: How dare you use that as the reason? I had a right to know I had a grandchild.

Brazil: A right? Are you serious? Don't you think Mystery has a right to know who his real mother is? I somewhat envy him, you know. All I went through growing up, I wish you would have given me away instead.

Before Diane got a chance to say anything, there was a knock at the door. Brazil went to answer. It was Ivy.

Brazil: Come on in. I will go get Ivan.

Ivy was surprise to see Diane. She knew Diane, but they never kept in touch after Brazil left. Brazil made her promise that.

Ivy: Hey, Ms. Diane.

Diane: You know when you were dating my son in school, I used to think you were the best thing that could have happened to him. Now I see I was wrong. How could you not tell me about my grandchild? What kind of person are you?

Ivy: We did what we thought was best for our son.

Brazil came from the back with Ivan who was asleep.

Brazil: He was complaining about his stomach, so I gave him some medicine.

Ivy: Okay, I will be staying with my father. I will call you tomorrow. You both have a good night.

Ivy left.

Diane: I think I will go back to the hospital and check on my friend. I am telling you, stay away from Mystery.

On the next episode, the dinner between Brazil and Alexandria takes place.

EPISODE 7

Brazil was up early looking through files when his business phone rang. "Hello, Brazil Private Investigator."

Client: Yes, I got your number off the Internet. I'm trying to find someone and was wondering if you can help.

Brazil: Of course, my rates are $1,000. I will need $500 up front to get started. Is this okay with you?

Client: Yes, money is not an issue.

Brazil: Okay, but do be aware that sometimes the end results are not always what the client wants to hear. Sometimes, I find people dead or alive. I don't like to get my client's hopes up, but I will do everything I can to find whoever you are looking for. Understand?

Client: I understand.

Brazil: Okay, I just need to get some information from you. Tell me who you are looking for and how do you know them.

Client: I need you to find my wife and child. They have been missing for almost a year now. I have been to everyone I know, and no one has been able to find them. You are my last hope.

Brazil: Okay, fax me a picture of your wife and child. I need a list of any living family members, close friends, last credit card statements, and vehicles, if she was driving one, and anything else you think can help me. The smallest thing may help. Also you can pay the upfront fee online.

Client: Okay, I will send this over right away.

They hung up, and Brazil got ready for his dinner with Alexandria.

At the Hospital

Mystery and Diane had stayed up late talking. He had told her all about his life with his mom, not knowing he was actually talking to his real mother. Diane told him about the time when she and Gloria was growing up and how she raised her. Gloria was a good motherly figure for Diane, but Diane just got with the wrong crowd and wanted to live her own life. They learned a lot about each other, except for the most important, and Diane was not about to let him know.

The doctor came in.

Doctor: How are you both doing?

Diane: We are good. Any change with my sister?

Doctor: I'm afraid not. We have done everything we can, but there is no response to anything.

Mystery just lowered his head.

Diane: Thanks, Doctor.

Doctor: I am leaving for the day, but I am always on call if anything changes.

He left. Diane went over to Mystery and hugged him.

Diane: I don't think that she is going to wake up, baby.

Mystery: I know. I'm just not ready to let her go yet.

Diane: I know. Me either, but do you think she would want to be laid up like this. Just think about it. I'm with you no matter what decision you make. I'm going to run some errands and will be back later, okay?

Mystery: Okay.

Mystery begins to talk to his mom. "Mom, I love you and don't know what to do. I'm not ready to be without you. I'm not that strong." He started crying. "I am sorry for all the pain I caused you growing up. I am sorry for saying you are no mother of mine. I was mad and didn't mean it. I will do anything. Just wake up, Momma, please." He held her hand and just stared at her.

All of a sudden, Brazil crossed his mind. He needed to talk to him and find out as much as possible about him and their mother before he made any kind of decision.

Doctor's House

Ivy had dinner all done. Her brothers had agreed to come over. She was in the kitchen getting everything set for when her dad got home when someone came through the door. "Who is that," she said.

Her brother Clay popped in the kitchen. "It's me."

Ivy: Heyyyyy.

They ran and gave each other a big hug. Clay was two years younger than Ivy and the baby. He was short, a little stocky, and a little feminine. He was gay and came out when he was a teenager. They all accepted it, but their older brother Malik. Even though they all accepted it, Clay never brought anyone he was dating around just to keep down confusion.

Clay: How you been, sis? I was so happy to hear from you.

Ivy: I've been well. We have so much to catch up on.

Clay always talked to Ivy about his love life. Since their mother passed, he always went to her for advice. There was a knock at the door. Ivy yelled come in as Clay and she walked in the living room. It was Malik. Malik was a tall muscular guy. He was also married with two kids of his own.

Ivy: Hey, big brother.

Malik: What's up? I missed you.

Malik gave her a kiss and hug. He looked at Clay without smiling.

Malik: Clay.

Clay: Malik.

No other words were exchanged between them. Ivy could see the tension and was wondering what could have taken place for this to happen. She will have to find out while she was here.

Ivy: So Dad should be pulling up any minute now. Malik, are you still working at the police station?

Malik: Yep, don't plan on going anywhere.
Ivy: What about you, Clay?
Clay: Still in school.
Malik made a grunt sound.
Clay: You have something to say, Malik?
Malik: Oh, I have a lot to say.
Ivy: Guys, come on now. Dad is pulling up.

A few minutes later, the doctor walked through the door. He hasn't had all his family under the same roof since his wife died. He was lost for words. He just stared at his children.

Alexandria's Place

Brazil and Alexandria had finished eating dinner. She asked him not to get into anything over dinner. "Let's just eat and talk afterwards." They made their way to the living room.

Brazil: Sean, I apologize for what happened the last time I was here. I honestly didn't know you were conversing with us both. I found out about my brother when I was eighteen. My mother told me the reason behind her giving him away and wanted me to stay away from him, but I couldn't. I had to get to know my brother. I just didn't want him to find out about me the way he did.

Alexandria: No problem. Mystery thought I was crazy, and I had to prove it to him. I'm sorry I tricked you over like that.

Brazil: It's cool. I'm kind of glad it's out now. Speaking of Mystery, I think you should know his mom had a heart attack and is in the hospital.

Alexandria: Oh no, I didn't know. I will give him a call later and check on him. You know, I realize I know nothing about you.

Brazil: Well, I used to work at Emory, but then, I started my own PI business. I have an ex-wife and a son, Ivy and Ivan. That's about it. Oh, and I have a big crush on you.

Even though Alexandria came clean with Mystery about her being a woman, she still needed to keep up the charade with Brazil.

Alexandria: Come on, Brazil, that's not possible. You are not gay.

Brazil: You are right. I'm not, but you are not either.

Alexandria was confused by that statement, and it showed by her facial expression.

Brazil continued.

Brazil: I know you are a woman, Sean. My question is, why is such a beautiful woman disguising herself as a guy?

Alexandria could not believe this. He knew the truth about her.

On the next episode, Brazil gets shocking and disturbing news.

EPISODE 8

Alexandria: Excuse me, what did you say?

Brazil: Come on, Sean, let us be honest. You don't have to lie to me. I like you.

Alexandria: I'm embarrassed. How did you know?

Brazil pointed at the window. "I've known now for a while, but I see I can't check things out anymore since you keep your blinds and curtains closed."

They both laughed.

Brazil: Now tell me the story behind this disguise? I promise not to judge.

Alexandria: Well, my real name is Alexandria. I have a husband and a child myself. One Friday night, almost a year ago, my husband came home drunk and woke me up just to fight. He put me in the hospital with a broken arm and busted nose that night.

Brazil: Did he go to jail?

Alexandria: No, because he is well-known. He would have gotten out that same night and did it again. The drinking was a serious problem he had, but when he did that to me, that did it. I knew I had to leave. He may have yelled and argued with me before, but he never went that far.

Brazil: Where was your son?

Alexandria: Jase was at a sleep over for the weekend. I was in the hospital for a few days. When I was released, I went straight and got my son and left the state. I didn't go by the house or anything. I didn't want to see him. I just drove until I got tired. Needless to say, I found my way to my sister's house in Florida. I left my son there and came to Georgia to start over. He will be coming to stay with me next month.

Brazil: Sorry to hear that. I'm glad we got everything out in the open. So can I take you out sometime as Alexandria and see where it takes us. We can get to know each other even more.

Alexandria: I would like that, Brazil. I really would.

Brazil: Okay, I got to go. Thanks for the dinner. It was good.

Before Brazil could stand, Alexandria reached over and gave him a kiss on the lips. She didn't know what came over her. She was finally able to talk to someone about her situation and feel comfortable about it and not having to disguise herself with them. They both stood up and hugged each other, and then he left.

Doctor's House

The family had just finished dinner. The doctor was so proud to have all his kids together.

Doctor: I'm so glad you are all here together, and I love you all.

They all said I love you back.

Doctor: Oh, before I forget. Clay, do you remember Mystery, Gloria's son?

Clay looked shocked and glanced over at Malik. Malik was staring at him like he had stolen something from him.

Clay: Yes, I remember him. We were good friends growing up until they stop coming to church.

Malik grunted.

Doctor: That's what I told Mystery. His mom had a heart attack and is in the hospital. He doesn't have any family here. I think you should drop by and see him. He can use a good surprise.

Malik: I bet he could.

Clay: I don't know, Dad. It's been some years since I last seen or talk to him.

Malik jumped up, to everybody's surprise, as if he was upset. "Dad, I got to get home. Dinner was good, sis, and I will talk to you later." He didn't say anything to Clay. Ivy walked him out.

Ivy: Malik, what was that. Dad is happy that we all are here.

Malik: I know, and I will call him later and start stopping by more often. I just can't be in the same room with that lying ass brother of yours.

Ivy: What you mean?

Malik: Ask him yourself. I'm out.

Malik left, and Ivy headed back to the kitchen.

Clay: I think I need to be leaving too, Dad. I got some studying to be doing. Ivy, call me tomorrow. Maybe we can get together and catch up.

Ivy: Sure, love you.

Clay: Love you too.

Clay left.

Ivy: Well, it's just me and you, Dad. What you want to talk about?

Doctor: My grandson's father.

Brazil's Place

Brazil had made it home, showered, and now sat at his desk looking through files. He was so happy with how the dinner date turned out and definitely the kiss. He feels that this could go to the next level. He was definitely going to try to take it there. They were open and honest with each other about everything.

He started going through the faxes from the new client when he came across a picture.

Brazil: What the . . . This can't be.

He was looking at a picture of Alexandria and a little boy.

On the next episode, Brazil has a decision to make, and Mystery gets a visitor.

EPISODE 9

Mystery's cell phone rang.

Mystery: Hello?

Alexandria: Hey, Mystery, it's Sean or Alexandria.

Mystery: What's up?

Alexandria: I just found out about your mother, and I am so sorry.

Mystery: Thanks.

Alexandria: Let me know if you need anything. I still care about you, Mystery.

Mystery: Okay I will, thanks. You know what, Sean, I think we should talk.

Alexandria: I agree, but I wasn't going to say anything because of what you're going through with your mom. You just let me know when.

Mystery: I will do that. By the way, what apartment number does Brazil live in? I need to talk to him.

Alexandria: 4022. Is everything all right?

Mystery: I just have some questions for him. I think I am entitled to that.

Alexandria: Yes, you are.

Mystery: I will talk to you later. Thanks for calling.

They hung up. Mystery was headed out the door. As soon as he opened it, Clay was standing there.

Mystery: Clay?

Brazil's Place

Brazil was stunned by the picture. His new client was looking for Alexandria and her son. He didn't know what to think or do. His client had paid him the $500 upfront fee to start the search. Brazil didn't have to do any search at all. He knew where his wife and child were. Now he was torn. He had just come clean with Alexandria about everything. He felt that they could have something between them, but he also had a job to do. He was professional at what he did. This was a hard decision. Should he tell the client where he could find his wife and child and hope Alexandria never finds out, or should he drop the client and pay his money back and hope it doesn't mess up his reputation? A reputation he spent years trying to build.

There was a knock at the door. "Come in." It was Diane.

Brazil: Look, Mother, I have a lot on my plate right now, and I don't have time to argue with you.

Diane: Look, we are going to talk about my grandson, whether you want to or not.

At the Hospital

Mystery: Clay, what are you doing here?

Clay walked in and hugged him and gave him a kiss.

Clay: I'm so sorry about your mom. Why didn't you call me?

Mystery: I wasn't going to bother you with my problems. Anyway, you have a lot of things to worry about yourself, don't you?

Clay: Just because we aren't together anymore don't mean I don't still love you. I made the wrong decision by picking Mason over you, and I see that. I never stopped loving you though.

Mystery (grinning): I remember when Mason, Malik, and I used to run the streets together. Everybody used to be scared of us.

Now look at all of us, we can't stand each other, but enough of all that. How did you find out?

Clay: My father. He thinks we are friends that haven't seen each other since we were little boys playing in church. He doesn't know we were in a relationship for a year.

Mystery: Good, because he is my mom's doctor, and I don't want any awkwardness. I am truly glad you came, but I need to step out for a minute and I am in a rush. I promise I will call you and stay in touch.

Clay: You better. Even if you don't, I will be calling you.

Clay leaned forward and kissed Mystery on the lips and left. Mystery left right behind him.

Brazil's Place

Diane: I want to see my grandson.

Brazil: Excuse me. You can't just walk in my house and demand anything. I will talk to Ivy and ask her to bring Ivan over tomorrow. You can see him then. How is Mystery?

Diane: What makes you think I have talked to him?

Brazil: Well, you said he is in the hospital with his mom, and you went to see your friend, so I thought maybe you both crossed paths again.

Diane: Well, we didn't. I told you I am staying away from him, and you should do the same.

Clay's Apartment

Clay had made it home later than normal. He shared his apartment with his boyfriend Mason. Mason was a tall, thuggish-looking guy built like a football player. When Clay went in, Mason was sitting in the recliner watching TV.

Clay: Hey.

Mason: Don't hey me. Where the hell you been?

Clay: I was at my dad's, then I went to see a friend in the hospital.

Mason stood up and walked toward Clay. Clay was frightened of him and scared to leave him as well. Mason stood in his face. "What friend?"

As soon as Clay said, "Mystery," Mason punched him in the face. Clay hit the floor. Mason grabbed him up by the neck. "This is why you are late, because you're out seeing him?" Clay tried to speak but couldn't. Mason punched him again in the stomach this time and dropped him. Clay couldn't do anything but cough and gasp for air. He didn't say anything because he knew it would only piss Mason off further.

Mason: Next time, call when you going to be late, otherwise have your ass in the house like you normally do. Oh, and don't ever let me catch you talking to Mystery.

Brazil's Place

Brazil: Mom, why you don't want Mystery to know the truth?

Diane: I just don't, okay? He will never understand why I gave him up, so it's best to just let him be.

Brazil: I think you should give him a chance. He don't want anything from either of us. He told me that himself.

Diane still was sticking to her decision.

Brazil: I'm sorry for not telling you about Ivan. I don't have a problem with you meeting and spending time with him now since you have gotten yourself together. Hold on, I have a picture you can have of him.

Diane: Thank you, son.

Brazil walked to the back to get the picture. There was a knock at the door.

Brazil: Get it, Mom.

Diane went to answer, and when she opened the door, she was shocked.

Diane: Mystery?

Mystery (stunned): Aunt Di? What are you doing here?

Walking from the back room, Brazil yelled out, "Who is it, Mom?" Then Brazil saw Mystery standing in the doorway.

On the next episode, Diane's secret is out.

EPISODE 10

Mystery: Did he just call you Mom?
　　Diane: Mystery, let me explain.
　　Mystery (raising his voice): Answer the question.
　　Brazil: Okay, calm down, Mystery.
　　Mystery: I'm not talking to you.
　　Mystery looked straight in Diane's eyes. "Are you his mother?" he asked.
　　Diane: Yes, yes, I am and yours.
　　Mystery took a deep breath. He said, "You have been lying this whole time, pretending to be my aunt."
　　Brazil: Hold on, your aunt? What is he talking about, Mom?
　　Diane: I will explain it later.
　　Brazil: No, you can explain it now. I am tired of all the lying.
　　Mystery: Oh, Brazil, you don't know. Your mother here has been pretending to be my aunt. She has been visiting my mom in the hospital every day. They are sisters.
　　Brazil: Mom, is this true? You told me a close friend of yours was in the hospital sick and that's the reason for your visit.
　　Mystery: Well, it looks like she's been lying to both of us.

Diane (yelling): Yes, it's true all right. It's true. I will explain it to you later Brazil, okay?

Mystery: No, you can explain it to him now. I'm done with this. I don't even want to be in the same room as you. You are a liar. You had me open up to you about a lot of things. I guess that was your way of trying to find out about your son you gave away, huh.

Diane went to reach for him.

Mystery (yelling): Don't touch me!

Diane: You don't know the whole story.

Mystery: There isn't a story. The bottom line is you gave me away and kept Brazil. You know what, I am glad you did, so thank you. I was raised by a loving and caring woman, one whom I consider my mother more than anything. Now I am going to go be with her, and I would appreciate if you don't come back tonight.

Without giving Diane a chance to say a word, Mystery left.

Clay's Apartment

Clay went to the bathroom to clean himself up. When he looked in the mirror, he could see his eye began to swell, and blood was dripping from his lip. He looked terrible. He has been going through this abuse for a while now. Everything he did was a problem. Clay was too scared to leave Mason. He tried before, and Mason beat him bad for it. He couldn't talk to Malik because they didn't get along and sure wasn't going to bring his dad into his love affair.

Clay's cell phone rings.

Clay: Hello.

Ivy: Hey, Clay. I'm going back to New Jersey tomorrow night. Let's go get breakfast in the morning.

Clay: Sure okay. What time?

Ivy: Text me your address, and I will be to pick you up at nine.

Clay: Okay, that's fine. I need to go. See you in the morning.

Clay hung up on Ivy.

Mason stepped in the bathroom. Clay froze up.

Mason: Who was that?

Clay: Ivy. She is picking me up in the morning to have breakfast before she goes back to New Jersey.

Mason stepped behind Clay and whispered into his ear, "You wouldn't be lying to me, would you?"

Clay (nervous): No, you can see my phone if you want.

Mason: Look at you. See what you make me do to you? You think I like this?

Clay: I'm sorry for being late. It will not happen again.

Mason: You're damn right it won't. Now clean yourself up and come to bed.

Mason went to bed, and Clay just stood there looking at himself in the mirror.

Doctor's House

Ivy: Dad, do you know what the problem is with Clay and Malik?

Doctor: I don't, baby. I just hope they can find a way to work whatever it is out. Now tell me about my grandson's father.

Ivy: Oh, Dad, he is a nice guy. We were college sweethearts who loved one another and had a beautiful child together. Long story short, we decided it would be best if we were just friends. He moved here to Atlanta and started his own private investigation business, which is successful, I must say.

Doctor: Is he a good father to Ivan?

Ivy: Oh yes, the best. He comes to New Jersey several times a year and visit. He stays in both of our lives. Now that he knows we may be moving here, he is thrilled because Ivan will be close to him.

Doctor: So is it official? Are you going to move back?

Ivy: Yes, I believe I am. My family needs me here.

Ivy grabbed her dad's hand. He was so happy she decided to move back.

Ivy: You're not going to get tired of me and Ivan being around every day, are you?

Doctor: Nonsense. I will also talk to the hiring staff at the hospital. I would love for you to work by my side as father and daughter.

Ivy: I will love that too. Now we're going back to New Jersey tomorrow. I'm going to take Ivan to Brazil tomorrow morning so he can spend time with him before we leave. So you have a good night. Love you.

Doctor: Good night, baby girl.
Ivy went upstairs to bed.

Brazil's Place

Brazil: Mystery is gone now, so explain yourself. You have a sister here and never told me.

Diane: I'm leaving. I am not going to get into this with you.

Brazil: If you leave without telling me the whole story, I promise you will never get to see your grandson again ever.

Diane: That's real big of you, son, to blackmail your own mother.

Brazil: Well, I'm tired of all the lies, but I mean it. You will not see him.

Diane: Okay, son, it is true. The lady in the hospital, the one whom Mystery thought was his mother, is my sister. Her name is Gloria. She raised me after our parents died. When I was a teenager, I ran away from home after a terrible fight with her. I saw her only once after that, and that was when she came and got me from the hospital when you both were born. I didn't tell you about her because I knew it would only help you find Mystery faster.

Brazil: Wow, so I have an aunt.

Diane: Yes. There, now you know the truth. I guess I will go back to my room since Mystery don't want me at the hospital tonight.

Brazil: Do you blame him?

Diane: No, but mark my word, tomorrow we will talk. He will hear what I have to say. Now that he knows the truth, he needs to know why.

Diane left.

On the next episode, Brazil makes a decision.

EPISODE 11

Brazil stayed up half the night and was up early this morning. He couldn't sleep after what all went down last night. Then on top of that, he had made his decision on what to do with his new client. So he decided to call him.

The phone rings.

Armon: Hello.

Brazil: May I speak with Armon Martinez?

Armon: Speaking.

Brazil: Armon, this is Brazil, the private investigator. I have some information about your wife and child.

Armon: Please tell me. Have you found them?

Brazil: I have found your wife. There are stipulations to getting this information though.

Armon: Oh thank you, thank you, thank you. What are the stipulations? Tell me. I don't care what they are. I will accept them. I'm so thankful you've found her.

Brazil: First, you have to pay the remaining fee before I can release anything to you.

Armon: Okay, I am doing that right now while we are on the phone.

Brazil: Second, you can't let the wife know how you found her or who found her for you. It's just company policy.

Armon: That's no problem. I do appreciate all you have done.

Brazil: I will be faxing the address to where you can find her as soon as your payment clears. This will close out your case. Best of luck.

Brazil hung up. He took a deep breath and hoped he made the right decision. He saw that the payment had cleared, so he faxed the information to Armon.

Armon received the fax. He was surprised to learn that Alexandria was in Atlanta. She didn't know it, but he had family there. He grinned to himself and said, "I got you now, and I'm coming for you, bitch."

Clay's Apartment

Clay was already up and ready. He put on shades so Ivy wouldn't notice the black swollen eye. Ivy called.

Clay: Hello.

Ivy: Hey, I'm downstairs.

Clay: Okay, I'm on my way down.

Clay got his keys and was heading out the door when Mason walked in the living room.

Mason: So you were going to leave without saying anything?

Clay: You were asleep, and I didn't want to wake you.

Mason: Bullshit, you weren't intending to. See, this is what I'm talking about.

Mason walked toward Clay. Clay started shaking.

Clay: Mason, please. Ivy is downstairs waiting for me.

Mason: Well, we don't want to keep her waiting, do we?

Mason opened the door for Clay and said, "Bring me some cigarettes back."

Clay: Okay, I will.

Clay slowly walked out the door and left. When he got downstairs, he ran to the car and jumped in.

Ivy: Whoa, why are you running like someone is behind you?

Clay said nervously and looked back, "I was just walking fast. Can we go?"

Ivy looked at Clay with a strange look and said, "Sure." Then they left.

At the Hospital

Mystery was asleep in the chair, dreaming. He could see his mother, Gloria, standing there in all white looking beautiful as ever. He couldn't get close to touch her. It's like she was standing in a distance but close enough for him to see her clearly.

Mystery: Mom?
Gloria: Yes, baby.
Mystery: How can this be?
Gloria: My sweet, sweet boy. You have to be strong now. It's time for you to be the man I raised you to be.
Mystery: Mama, I can't. I don't want to lose you. I'm sorry for being rude to you. I'm sorry for saying you're no mother of mine. I didn't mean that.
Gloria: Awww, baby, I know. I'm at peace now. You have to learn to open your heart up and accept love if it's there to be given. Don't close yourself off from the world. You have a family now.
Mystery: I don't need anybody but you.
Gloria: That's not true. You have family and friends that love you. Give them a chance for me, okay?
Mystery: Okay but—
Gloria: You will always be my son, Mystery. I will always love you no matter what.

Mystery could hear his name being called, and he could feel he was being shaken.

Gloria: I will always be with you in your heart. You are my boy, and I love you.

Gloria began to fade away from Mystery's sight.

Mystery: Mama, wait. Don't go. Mama!
Diane: Mystery, wake up. You're dreaming.

She was shaking him. Mystery slowly opened his eyes.

On the next episode, Clay comes clean with Ivy.

EPISODE 12

Ivy and Clay had made it downtown to a café. They decided to sit outside since the weather was nice.

Ivy: So, Clay, what is the deal with you and Malik?

Clay: I knew you were going to ask that. Where do I begin? Malik had two best friends, Mystery and Mason. I met Mystery at this club one night. We talked and became close. We started dating, and then it turned into a relationship. Even though Malik tolerated me being gay, he was not going to accept me being in a relationship with his best friend. He cut both me and his friend loose. Mystery and I was in a relationship for a year. Then one night, I lost it all.

Ivy: What happened?

Clay: Well, Malik had a birthday party last year. Everybody was drunk and having a good time. Even though he was not talking to me or Mystery, we still went to the party. I went to the bathroom, and Mason was in there. When Mason came out and saw me standing there, he just stared at me. I'm like, what is he staring at? All he did was grab me into the bathroom and start kissing me. I will say I didn't try to stop him because I always had a thing for him before Mystery, but Mason wasn't gay, so I left him alone. At least that's what I thought because he always had a girl. So I gave in to him. We didn't have sex but would have if Mystery hadn't caught us in the act.

Ivy: Ouch.

Clay: We were all drunk. There was this huge fight between Mason and Mystery. They turned the party out, and Malik was very pissed. Mystery broke it off with me that night, so I turned to Mason. He had a thing for me the whole time, and I didn't know it. Don't get me wrong. I begged Mystery to forgive me and give me another chance, but I had hurt him too deeply. But we are good now. We are really good friends. Now you see why me and Malik don't get along. He blames me for breaking up his friendship with both Mystery and Mason.

Ivy: How's your relationship with Mason?

Clay took his shades off.

At the Hospital

Mystery opened his eyes and saw Diane standing there.

Diane: I didn't mean to wake you, but you were dreaming and talking out loud.

Mystery: What are you doing here?

Diane: We need to talk.

Mystery stood up. "I think you talked enough last night," he said.

Diane: Well, I didn't, and I need to explain the situation to you. Now do you want to talk in here in front of her or go somewhere else? Either way, we are having this conversation.

Mystery: Waiting room.

They walked to the waiting room.

Mystery: Okay go ahead. I'm listening.

Diane: Before I got pregnant with you and Brazil, I was on drugs really bad. Any kind of drugs there was or I could get, I did it. I did whatever I had to do to get it. I have stolen, robbed people, even prostituted. I was out there, bad. That's why I ran away from home, from Gloria. Even though she raised me after our parents died, I wasn't going to bring what I was doing in her life.

Mystery: So you did her a favor by leaving?

Diane: I really do believe so. One night, I was prostituting, and I met these three guys. They had money and drugs, so I got in the car with them. We went to this motel, and you can imagine what happened from there. That was the night I got pregnant with you and Brazil. I didn't find out until a month later though.

Mystery: So you are telling me that our dad is one of three guys?

Diane: One of two. The third guy didn't have sex with me. He just wanted to get high.

Mystery: Did you even know either of them?

Diane: No, Mystery. You have to realize I didn't care who they were. I just wanted a fix, and I did whatever I had to do to get it.

Mystery: I still want to know why you gave me away.

Diane: When I got pregnant, that still didn't stop me from doing drugs. I still wanted it. This guy that I knew told me about this couple that wanted a baby but didn't want to go through the adoption agency. At this time, I had already learned that I was having twins, so this was perfect for me. They were willing to pay me $100,000 for one of my babies, so I agreed to it. You see how bad off I was? I agreed to sell my baby for money so I could get dope.

Mystery just stood there, listening.

Diane: When I gave birth, I decided to reach out and call Gloria. I hadn't talked to her in over a year. She rushed to the hospital and was actually happy to see me. When I told her what I agreed to, she was furious. She took it upon herself to call the couple and let them know that if they came to the hospital to try and buy a baby, she would call the cops. I was very upset with her for doing that. I told her I needed that money and I couldn't afford to take care of two babies. She agreed to take one of you and raise as her own. When you and Brazil were healthy enough to leave the hospital, Gloria came and got us. We went back home with her. She had three suitcases packed by the door. That's when she told me she was moving here to Atlanta. She didn't say why, but I knew she wanted to be far from me and my problems. She told me I could have the house and that she was leaving that night. That night, she picked you as her baby. She gave me an envelope and told me not to open it until she left. She loaded everything in the car and left with you. I never saw her again after that.

Mystery: What was in the envelope?
Diane: A $100,000 check.

At the Café

Ivy: Clay, oh my god, what happened?

Clay: Mason happened.

Ivy: Mason did this? Did you call the police?

Clay: Ivy, seriously? How would that look? And besides, Malik works there.

Ivy: So what, and it would look like someone needing help. It doesn't matter if you're in a gay or straight relationship. No one deserves to be beaten. How long have this been going on?

Clay: I don't know, a while now. He gets so angry at times.

Ivy: I'm calling Malik.

Clay: No, no, Ivy. I will take care of it.

Ivy: You better because if you don't. I will get the police involved.

Clay: It will be okay. Now come on and take me back. You have a plane to go catch.

They left. When Clay made it home, he was hoping that Mason had left, but he wasn't. As soon as he stepped in the apartment, Mason asked, "Did you get the cigarettes?"

Clay: I'm sorry I forgot.

Mason raised his voice. "You forgot, you forgot. You might as well turn right around and go get it like I told your ass."

Clay: Okay, okay, I will be right back.

Clay went to pick up his car keys.

Mason: Leave the damn keys.

Clay: How am I supposed to get to the store?

Mason: Walk your big ass there. Teach you to not forget the next time.

Clay: Mason, it's starting to rain now, and the store is five miles away.

Mason: I don't give a damn, and I'm not going to tell you again.
Clay: I am not walking. That is too far.
Mason stood up. "What did you say to me?" he said.

On the season finale, Mystery lets Gloria go. A terrible tragedy strikes.

EPISODE 13—
SEASON FINALE

Ivy had made it to Brazil's house to pick up Ivan. Before she went in, she decided to call Malik.

Malik's phone rings.

Malik: Hey, sis. What's going on?

Ivy: Just letting you know that I am leaving for New Jersey today. I'm going to go get things squared away before my move back.

Malik: That's great. I'm so glad you're moving back home.

Ivy: Yes, me too. Now I need for you to go check on Clay today.

Malik: Ivy, why would I do that? You know we don't get along. I stay out of his way, and he stays out of mine.

Ivy: First, he is your brother, and he told me everything that went down.

Malik: Well, there you go. You know why we don't talk.

Ivy: Did you know Mason has been beating him?

Malik: What? I don't believe that. Clay will say anything to make himself get sympathy from others.

Ivy: Well, it's true. I saw him today, and his eye is closed up. He told me this has been going on for a while. He doesn't want to get the police involved because you work there, which is no excuse, if you ask me. Will you go check on him today for me?

Malik: Ivy, I am not going to get involved with that.

Ivy: Are you serious? He is your brother. On top of that, you are an officer of the law. You will stand back and let him get hurt like that? I don't want to call Dad, so I am asking you.

Malik: Okay, okay, I will go by there. I don't want Dad to know about this either. I'm sure it's not a big deal.

Ivy: Thank you. I'm going to pick up Ivan and head to the airport. I will see you when I get back. Love you.

Malik: Love you too, sis. Bye.

Ivy went upstairs to Brazil's place and knocked. Brazil came to the door with Ivan right behind.

Brazil: Hey, he is all ready.

Ivy: Hey, baby, you ready?

Ivan: No, I want to stay with Dad.

Brazil: What if I come to the airport with you and watch you take off?

Ivan: Okaaaay.

Brazil: Ivy, I know you have to turn the rental back in, so I will just follow you there, and Ivan can ride with me.

Ivy: Okay with me. Let's go.

They left for the airport.

Clay's Apartment

Mason: What did you say to me?

Clay: I'm not going to walk, Mason. It's starting to rain.

Mason walked toward Clay and stood in his face. Clay just lowered his head.

Mason: Say it again.

Clay: I'm—

Mason slapped him. Clay ran into the kitchen and picked up a knife.

Clay: I'm not going to do this with you.

Mason: Oh, so you're going to cut me? Well, come on, do it!

Mason walked toward him. Clay's hand was shaking.

Mason: Go ahead. Cut me.

Mason got in his face. Clay held the knife to Mason's stomach.

Clay: Please, Mason.

Mason: Do it!

Clay was terrified because he knew what was coming if he didn't. Mason grabbed his hand and took the knife.

Mason: You always were a weak bitch. I'm going to show you what to do with this knife.

Mason put the knife to Clay's neck and pressed it.

Clay: Mason, stop please.

Clay started crying. Mason pressed the knife harder until he cut the skin enough for it to bleed. Blood rolled down Clay's neck.

Mason: Don't you ever threaten me unless you mean it.

Mason put the knife down and slapped him again. There was a knock at the door.

Mason: Who is it?

Malik: Police, open up.

Mason told Clay he better not say anything about this. If he did, he would regret it. Mason went to the door and opened it.

Mason: Malik, surprise to see you.

Malik: Mason, where is Clay?

Mason: I will go get him.

Mason closed the door. He went to the kitchen and got the knife.

Mason: Your brother wants to see you. Say one thing, and I will hurt you. Don't make me hurt you.

Clay wiped the blood from his neck and put on his shades, and they both walked to the door. Mason was right behind him with the knife pointed in his back where he could feel it. Clay opened the door.

Clay: Malik, what are you doing here?

Malik: Ivy wanted me to come over and check on you. Is everything okay here?

Clay (nervous): Everything's fine.

Malik: Are you sure? I'm here as an officer, not your brother now. So I'm asking you again, is everything okay here?

Mason: I think he's already answered that question.

Malik: And I'm asking it again.

Mason poked Clay in the back with the knife.

Clay: Yes, everything is okay.

Malik: Clay, take off the shades.

Clay: Malik.

Malik: Now, Clay.

Clay slowly took off his shades. Malik could see Ivy was telling the truth about Clay's eye.

Malik: What happened to your eye? Did Mason do this?

At the Airport

Brazil, Ivy, and Ivan made it to the airport and went to the terminal where they will be departing from.

Ivy: Here we go. Coastal Airlines Flight 202.

Ivan: Daddy, I don't want to go. Can I stay with you?

Brazil: You have to go look out for your mom while I'm not there. You both will be back real soon. Tell you what, when you get back, I'm going to take you to Six Flags. How that sounds?

Ivan: Promise?

Brazil: I promise.

The attendant called for boarding over the PA.

Brazil: Okay that's you, guys. Give me a hug, lil man. I love you.

Ivan: I love you too, Daddy.

Brazil gave Ivy a hug and kiss on the cheek.

Ivy: See you soon.

Brazil said okay and watched them board, then he left.

At the Hospital

Diane: Now, Mystery, you know the whole truth. I hope one day you can forgive me.

Mystery: My mama taught me to forgive, so yes, I forgive you, but make no mistake, I will never forget.

Diane: That's all I can ask of you. Thank you.

Mystery dropped his head.

Mystery: I'm ready to let Mama go.

Diane: Are you sure?

Mystery: Yes, I spoke to her today, and she is at peace now. Can you go get the doctor and bring him back to the room?

Diane: Of course, baby.

Diane went to get the doctor, and Mystery went back to the room. He just stood there staring at her. Diane and the doctor came in.

Doctor: Your aunt told me you made a decision.

Taking a deep breath, Mystery replied, "Yes. I want to take her off the machine."

Doctor: Are you sure?

Mystery: Yes, I'm sure.

Doctor: Okay, is there anything you both want to say before I turn it off?

Diane gave her sister a kiss and whispered to her, "I will do right by Mystery, I promise. I love you."

Mystery gave her a kiss on the forehead and held her hand. "I love you, Mom."

The doctor took the breathing tube out of her mouth, then he turned off the machine. Diane began to cry. They all watched the heart monitor as it decreased—90, 80, 70, 60, 50, 40, 30, 20, 10, 0.

Alexandria's Place

Alexandria was in such a good mood today for some reason. She guessed because she had talked to her son Jase and knew he would be coming to stay with her next week. She couldn't wait to see him as she missed him so much. She wanted to share the news with Brazil. She and Brazil had become close. He made her feel good about herself. She didn't have to pretend to be anyone else but her with him. She had cooked a nice dinner and decided to take him a plate just to show him she was thinking about him. She got dressed up as herself, Alexandria, to go see him. She got her keys and dinner plate and was heading out the door. As soon as she opened the door, Armon was standing there. She dropped the plate. She couldn't speak. She could see the evil look in his eyes.

Armon: Hello, Alexandria. Did you actually think I wouldn't find you?

Armon stepped in as she backed away. He closed the door and locked it.

Brazil's Place

Brazil had made it home from the airport. He sat down on the sofa and turned on the television. He always hated leaving his son. He laid his head back and nodded off. An hour had passed when he was awakened by a special alert siren coming from the television. He lifted his head and turned up the television.

Newsman: This is a special report. Flight 202 with Coastal Airlines has crashed. Authorities on the scene have confirmed that there are no survivors.

Brazil slowly stood up. He couldn't believe what he was seeing. He was sure he misheard.

Newsman: This is a terrible tragedy. Flight 202 with Coastal Airlines has crashed.

Brazil whispered to himself, eyes filling up with tears, "Ivan. Ivy." Falling to his knees and grabbing his head, Brazil yelled out, "Nooooooooooooooooooo!"

To be continued.

Part 3

EPISODE 1

Brazil just laid there on the floor. He was out of it. He couldn't believe his son and ex-wife were dead. All he could think about was Ivan asking if he could stay with him. If he'd only told him yes, things would be different. He called Ivy's cell phone several times just to hear her and Ivan's voice on her voice mail.

Brazil had tried to call the police station earlier but couldn't get through. He knew it was going to be impossible to get through with all the other families calling in about the crash. He began to feel that there was nothing for him to live for. Although Ivan never lived with him full time, he was his everything. His phone began to ring. He saw it was his mother Diane. He just let it rang and stayed balled up on the floor crying.

Mystery's Place

Mystery had made it home. Diane followed him there as she didn't want him to be alone. She had tried to call Brazil to let him know about Gloria's passing, but there was no answer. Instead of leaving a voice mail, she figured she would just stop by later and tell him in person.

Diane: Mystery, is there anything you need for me to do?

Mystery replied in a low voice, "No, I am just going to go upstairs and go to bed."

Diane: Oh, okay sure. I will be here when you get up in the morning, okay?

Mystery: Yeah, okay, whatever.

Mystery went upstairs and laid across his bed. He knew his life would never be the same now his mom was gone.

Diane started cleaning up. She had to keep herself busy. She remembered the promise she whispered to Gloria before she died about doing right by Mystery. She was intending to do just that.

Clay's Apartment

Malik: Clay, I asked you a question. Did Mason do this to your face?

Mason: How are you going to come to my house and accuse me of something? You're lucky you're wearing that uniform.

Malik, trying to get pass Clay, replied, "Oh, you're threatening me?"

Clay: Wait, wait, Malik. No, he didn't do it. I fell getting out the shower and hit my face on the corner of the sink. You know how clumsy I am.

Mason: There you have it. Now leave my house.

Looking dead at Mason, Malik said, "This is Clay's apartment, and don't you forget that. You're just here free loading off of him. You need to get you a job and help him."

Clay: Malik, everything is fine, okay?

Malik: Look, I don't believe you, but I will leave it alone for now. If you need me, call me.

Clay: Okay I will.

Malik left. Clay closed the door and went into the bedroom, not saying a word to Mason.

Alexandria's Place

Alexandria: Get out.

Armon: Oh no, no, no. We have some unfinished business to discuss.

Alexandria: How did you find me?

Armon: You need not worry your pretty little head about that. You know how resourceful I am.

Alexandria: What do you want?

Armon: Now that is the question. Where is my son?

Alexandria: I will never tell you that. Now get out.

Armon just stood there, looking at her with this angry look.

Alexandria: I'm calling the police.

Alexandria went to go for the phone.

Armon: You're not calling anybody.

She looked up and saw Armon had a gun in his hand. That made her nervous because all the time that has passed, she didn't know what he could be capable of.

Alexandria: Armon, what are you doing with that?

Armon: What do you think I'm going to do with it? I was hoping not to have to use it.

He cocked the gun.

Alexandria: Armon, don't.

Armon: Don't what? See, let me tell you what is going to happen right now. You are going to tell me where my son is, and then we are going to go get him.

Alexandria: I can't do that.

Armon: See, that is not an option. Alexandria, I will kill you right here and disappear where no one will find me. You know me, and you know I can.

He was telling the truth about that. He was an ex-police officer and ex-marines. She felt that she didn't have a choice.

Alexandria: Jase is not here in Atlanta. He is in Florida with my sister.

Armon: I should have known Adriana would be in on this. She never liked me anyway. Okay, so call Adriana and have her bring him home. We can have a little family reunion when she gets here.

Alexandria: Armon, please let Jase be. He is happy there.

Cutting her off, Armon yelled and pointed the gun to her head, "Call your sister, or I swear I will pull this trigger. You think you can take my son away from me for almost a year and there be no consequences. Call her now!"

Alexandria: Okay, okay, I'm calling.

Armon: Don't tell her I'm here either.

She dialed Adriana and the phone rang.

Adriana: Hello.

Alexandria: Hey, sis, how is everything?

Adriana: Everything is okay. You want to talk to Jase?

Alexandria: No, no, I actually need a huge favor.

Adriana: Okay, what is it?

Alexandria: I need you to bring Jase to me tomorrow.

Adriana: Are you sure? I thought you were going to wait until next week.

Alexandria: I was, but everything is okay here now so why wait.

Adriana: I mean okay, if you want. I will pack him up tonight, and we will head out in the morning.

Alexandria: Thanks, sis. I got to go. Love you.

Alexandria hung up, not giving Adriana a chance to say anything.

Armon with a smirk on his face said, "I can't wait to see my sister-in-law."

Brazil's Place

Hours had passed. Brazil was still lying on the floor. He looked at his phone and noticed Diane had called three times. He figured she knew about Ivy and Ivan and wanted to talk. He didn't feel like being bothered. All of a sudden, there was a knock at his door. He took a deep breath. He just wanted to be left alone. There was another knock. Brazil got up and went to answered it. When he opened the door, he couldn't believe it. It was Ivy and Ivan.

On the next episode, Brazil is overjoyed to have Ivan and Ivy back.

EPISODE 2

Brazil could not believe his eyes. Ivy was standing there holding Ivan. He had fallen asleep on their way back to Brazil's house. Brazil just stood there in shock, and then, he grabbed Ivy and Ivan and just hugged them. He started to cry all over again.

Ivy surprised by the way Brazil was acting said, "What's wrong? We haven't been gone two hours good."

Brazil didn't say anything. He just held on to them both.

Ivy: Brazil, what is going on?

Brazil: Oh, I'm sorry. You haven't heard?

Ivy handed Ivan over to him.

Ivy: Heard what?

Brazil: Let me lay him down, and I will tell you.

Brazil went and laid Ivan on his bed, then came back. Ivy could tell something was wrong.

Brazil: I've been calling your cell.

Ivy: It went dead on me at the airport. What is going on with you? You look like you have been drinking or something.

Brazil: Did you miss your flight?

Ivy: Not really. The plane was overbooked so they asked if anyone would volunteer to take a tomorrow flight instead. I volunteered because I knew Ivan wasn't ready to leave yet, and he was upset. I got two free plane tickets for volunteering though.

Brazil: So you haven't heard what happened?

Ivy: No, what happened?

Brazil: Ivy, that plane crashed.

Ivy: What?

Alexandria's Place

Alexandria: Armon, what are you planning to do?

Armon: I just want to see my son. You have kept him from me for almost a year.

Alexandria: I know, but do you blame me. You were becoming this person I didn't know anymore especially when you were drinking.

Armon: Are you trying to justify taking my son away?

Alexandria: No, but—

Armon: Just shut up! They will be here tomorrow, then we will go from there. You can go to bed, if you want. I am not going anywhere. I will be right here on this sofa.

As Alexandria was heading to the bedroom, Armon spoke, "Oh, Alexandria, don't try to leave during the night, okay. I really wouldn't advise that for your sake."

She went on to the bedroom and closed the door.

Mystery's Place

Diane had just finished cleaning up downstairs. She went upstairs and looked in on Mystery. She saw he was asleep. She went back downstairs and laid on the sofa. She didn't realize how tired she was until she actually laid down. She needed to rest as well. She knew it would be a hard day tomorrow for her and especially for Mystery trying to make funeral arrangements. She would be there as long as Mystery needed her.

Brazil's Place

Ivy: Did you just say the plane crashed?

    Brazil nodded.

    Ivy: The one I decided not to take?

    Brazil: Yes. I thought you and Ivan were on it. I saw you both board.

    Ivy: We did board but got off after I volunteered. I would have called you, but I told you, my phone had died.

    Ivy stood up in disbelief.

    Ivy: All those innocent people, any survivors?

    Brazil: No. I was out of it. I'm so grateful that you both got off. I want you both to stay here tonight. I need for you both to stay.

    Ivy: Of course.

    Brazil: You can have my bed with Ivan. I will sleep out here. You should call your dad and brothers to let them know you are okay.

    Ivy: Yes, you're right. I will do that now.

    Ivy walked to the back room. Brazil was so relieved. He got down on his knees and gave thanks to the man above.

On the next episode, Mystery makes funeral arrangement. Armon meets his son.

EPISODE 3

The next morning, Ivy was up early. She kept thinking about the fact that she and Ivan could have been on that plane. She was truly thankful and blessed to be alive. Ivan was still sleeping, so she left him in the bed and went to the living room. She saw that Brazil was already up sipping on coffee.

Ivy: Morning.
Brazil: Good morning. How did you sleep?
Ivy: I couldn't, considering I could have been dead right now.
Brazil: I know, but you aren't, thank God. Have a seat. I need to tell you something.
Ivy: Please no more bad news. I couldn't deal with it right now.
Brazil: No, it's actually some good news.
Ivy: Good, what is it?
Brazil: You remember the reason I left New Jersey to come to Atlanta, right?
Ivy: Of course I do. You wanted to find your brother.
Brazil grinned.
Ivy: Wait a minute. Did you find him?
Brazil: Yes, I did, and he is here in Atlanta.

MYSTERY

Mystery's Place

Mystery got up and got dressed. He knew he had a lot to do today. He had to make phone calls, funeral arrangements, etc. He and Gloria had talked about if something like this ever happened what she wanted. She wanted to be buried as soon as possible. She didn't want everyone's pain to linger. Mystery was going to do all he could to make that happen. He went downstairs and saw that Diane was sleeping on the sofa. He went to the kitchen and made himself a bowl of cereal. As soon as he sat down at the table, Diane walked in.

Diane: Good morning, Mystery.

Mystery: Good morning. I saw you were asleep and didn't want to wake you.

Diane: Oh, that's okay. I don't sleep hard at all.

Mystery: I was wondering if you would come with me to the funeral home. I don't think I can do this by myself.

Diane: Of course I will baby, whatever you need.

Mystery: I want the funeral to be tomorrow at two o'clock. Mama didn't want to be out long at all, and she wanted a private service with a few friends.

Diane: Okay, if you make me a list of names, I will call everybody for you if you want.

Mystery: Okay but let us go ahead and head to the funeral home first.

Diane: Okay, sure, let me just get dressed.

Diane was happy that Mystery was letting her help. He didn't have to after what all he had learned. Diane got dressed, and they both headed out.

Malik's House

Malik was off today. He didn't like getting involved in Clay's business, but it was clear he was being abused. Ivy was right. Even though he didn't like what Clay did to him in the past, he still cared for his brother. He just never showed it. He couldn't help Clay if he didn't want it. Malena saw that something was on Malik's mind. Malena was Malik's wife. They have two kids, Melanie, fourteen, and Ashley, ten. Malena used to be a schoolteacher but decided to be a stay-at-home mom after her second child. Malik never understood why, but he agreed to it to make her happy.

Malena: Hey, babe, what's going on? You tossed and turned all last night.

Malik: I went to see Clay last night before I came home.

Malena: That's good. I'm glad you both are talking again. How is he?

Malik: Mason is physically abusing him.

Malena: Oh no, are you sure?

Malik: Yes, his eye was swollen shut. He said Mason didn't do it, but I know he did because Ivy told me. Clay confessed everything to her.

Malena: What are you going to do?

Malik: I can't do anything. Clay will not admit to it. One thing's for sure, it better not keep happening.

Brazil's Place

Ivy: Brazil, that is great. Have you talked to him?

Brazil: Yes, but it's a long story. He is dealing with a lot right now as well.

Brazil's cell phone rang.

Brazil: Hello.

Diane: Brazil, it's mother. I've been calling you.

Brazil: I know they both are fine.

Diane: What are you talking about?

Brazil: Aren't you calling about Ivan and Ivy?

Diane: No. What happened?

Brazil didn't want to get into it over the phone. He will just tell her about it when he sees her.

Brazil: Oh, never mind. I thought you were calling about something else. What's going on?

Diane: Gloria died yesterday.

Brazil: Awww, man. How's Mystery?

Diane: He's making it. The funeral will be tomorrow at two o'clock. He wanted me to call everyone and let them know. It's going to be a small service.

Brazil: Okay, I will be there. I will visit him later today, if that's okay.

Diane: The secret is out now about me being his mother. I think it will be nice for him to hear from you.

Brazil: Okay, I will do that. Talk to you later.

Brazil hung up and turned to Ivy and said, "So would you like to go meet my twin brother?"

Alexandria's Place

Alexandria was in the bedroom, watching television when there was a knock at the front door. Armon bust in the bedroom.

Armon: Come answer the door. I will wait in here and don't try anything.

Alexandria went to answer the door. She saw it was Adriana, Max, and Jase. As soon as she opened the door, Jase ran through and jumped in her arms.

Jase: Mom!

Alexandria: Hey, baby. Oh, I missed you so much.

Adriana and Max came in and gave her a hug.

Alexandria: Hey, you guys. How was the trip?

Max: It wasn't too bad. Adriana slept all the way. Jase kept me company while I was driving, didn't you, little man?

Jase: Yep.

Adriana: Alexandria, can you tell us what was the big rush.

As soon as she said that, Armon came from the bedroom.

Armon: She wanted to surprise you.

Adriana and Max were both stunned to see him.

Adriana: What are you doing here? Alexandria, what is he doing here?

Armon: I am here to see my son.

Jase: Dad?

Armon: Yes, son, it is me. Come give me a hug.

Jase grabbed onto Alexandria harder and said, "No."

Armon (surprised): What do you mean no?

He knew something wasn't right because Jase and him were really close before Alexandria left with him almost a year ago. Armon looked at Adriana and Max.

Armon: What have you been telling my son about me?

On the next episode, Ivy meets Mystery. Armon makes serious threats.

EPISODE 4

Mystery and Diane had made it back home. They had been out all day, making the funeral arrangements and getting everything squared away for tomorrow.

Mystery: I want to thank you for helping me today with all this. I never had to go through something like this before.

Diane: Oh, it's not a problem at all. Gloria and I may have had our differences, but she still was my sister, and I loved her. Now I need to go make a run then after I will head back to the hotel.

Mystery: Mama is gone now, and even though I haven't gotten over the fact that you have lied to me about being my biological mother, she would want you here. I would like it if you stayed here until all this is over.

Diane was so happy to hear that. She accepted. She could work on getting close to Mystery during this time.

Diane: That means a lot, Mystery. Okay, so I will make my run and go get my things from the hotel and be back as soon as I can.

Mystery: Okay.

Diane left.

Clay's Apartment

Clay's cell phone rings. It's his dad.

Clay: Hey, Dad, what's up?

Doctor: Hey, son, did your sister call you?

Clay: Yes, she did. I'm still shocked that her plane went down. I'm so grateful she wasn't on it.

Doctor: Yes, I know, me too. Have you talked to Mystery lately?

Clay looked around to make sure Mason wasn't eavesdropping and sneaking up on him.

Clay: No, not in a few days.

Doctor: His mom died.

Clay: Oh no, I didn't know that. I will give him a call and check on him.

Doctor: That would be nice. He can use a good friend right now. Also after all this with Ivy, I want to have all my family over for dinner real soon. That includes whomever you're dating as well.

Clay: Dad, come on now.

Doctor: No, I am serious. You know I have never judged you. You are my son, and I love you. I want you to be happy. I want that for all my children.

Clay could only think about Mystery. Mystery was the only one that truly made him happy.

Clay: Just let me know when the dinner is, and I will be there.

Doctor: Okay, son, I love you.

Clay: Love you too, Dad.

They hung up. Clay immediately dialed Mystery.

Mystery: Hello.

Clay: Hey, Mystery, it's Clay. I'm so sorry to hear about your mom.

Mystery: Thank you. The service is going to be tomorrow at two o'clock if you would like to come.

Clay: Of course I will be there.

Clay walked to the bathroom and lowered his voice.

Clay: Mystery, I am here for you. I care about you so much.

Mystery: That's sweet of you to say. I care about you too. How's everything going with you?

Clay: Oh, don't worry about me. I would like to focus on you right now. I don't want you to think that you are alone. I will always be here for you.

Mystery: It's really good to hear your voice.

There was a knock at Mystery's door.

Mystery: Someone is knocking at my door.

Clay: Okay, go ahead, and I will see you tomorrow. I love you.

Clay hung up and didn't realize that Mason was standing behind him.

Mason: Who are you saying I love you to?

Mystery's Place

Mystery went to answer the door. It was Brazil, Ivy, and Ivan.

Brazil: Hey, Mystery. We come to pay our respects. Can we come in?

Mystery: Sure, come in.

Ivy could not believe the resemblance. Ivan was kind of confused himself.

Brazil: Mystery, this is my ex-wife and son, Ivy and Ivan.

Mystery shook Ivy's hand.

Mystery: Nice to meet you.

Ivy: I am so sorry about your mom.

Mystery: Thanks. It's nice to meet you too, Ivan.

Ivan: Why do you look just like my dad?

Brazil: Hey, lil man, this man here is my twin brother, your uncle.

Ivan: Twin brother?

Ivy: Yes, baby, it's when two babies are born at the same time.

Ivy turned to Mystery.

Ivy: I'm sorry about the questions.

Mystery: Oh, no problem. I think it's been a shock for all of us. Would you all like something to drink?

Brazil and Ivy: No, thank you.

Mystery: How about you, Ivan? I have some juice in the fridge.

Ivan: Can I, Mom?

Ivy: Sure.

They all went to the kitchen. Mystery poured some juice for Ivan. Ivan sat at the table and begins to drink it.

Mystery: I appreciate you both for stopping by. Brazil, did your mom tell you about the service?

Brazil: Yes, she called me last night. Ivy and I both will be there.

Mystery: Okay, thanks. Oh, I think you should know I asked her to stay here.

Brazil: You did what?

Alexandria's Place

Armon: What have you been telling my son?

Adriana: We haven't been telling Jase anything about you. Get over yourself.

Armon: Well, you both can leave now. Alexandria and I can raise our own son now.

Adriana: We are not going anywhere. You are.

Armon: Oh really?

Armon opened his coat up revealing the gun to Adriana and Max.

Armon: Don't make this situation ugly. My son and his mother have a lot of catching up to do.

Alexandria walked toward Adriana and Max.

Alexandria: It's ok. I will be ok.

Max: Are you sure?

Alexandria: Yes.

Adriana: Okay but we are not leaving town. We are going to check into a hotel right down the street just in case.

Armon: It really doesn't matter where you stay as long as you leave here. Oh, and don't try to get the police involved. I don't think you want your sister to go to jail for kidnapping.

Adriana: Go to hell. Let's go, Max.

They both left.

Armon: Now I have my family back.

On the next episode, Clay tries explains himself to Mason.

EPISODE 5

Alexandria: Jase, do Mommy a favor. Go watch TV in my room so I can talk to Daddy.

Jase: Okay.

Jase walked to the bedroom. Alexandria turned to Armon.

Alexandria: What do you mean you have your family back? You can't stay here.

Armon: Why not? You are my wife.

Alexandria: I don't want you in my life or Jase's. After what you did to me, do you blame me?

Armon: I am sorry for putting you in the hospital, but I am better now.

Alexandria: I don't care. I am not going to put Jase or myself through that.

Armon: Jase didn't even know what went on and for him to act like he just did with me tells me that your sister has told him something. I am going to find out what she did to turn him against me like that.

Alexandria: I don't know anything about that. Armon, you have to leave.

Armon: Let me tell you something. I will leave for now, but you will not keep me from my son anymore. I will be staying in Atlanta, so don't try to leave the state again. I have found you now, and just because I am not staying here, I will have someone watching you. Now call my son so I can say good-bye for now.

Alexandria was scared because she knew there was no running or escaping Armon this time. She really believed he had someone watching her. He was very resourceful and capable.

Alexandria: Jase, can you come here for a minute.

Jase came from the bedroom.

Jase: Yes, Mama.

Alexandria: Say good-bye to your dad.

Armon: Jase, I will be back to see you. I miss you so much. I love you no matter what you've heard.

Armon gave him a kiss on the head and left.

Malik's House

Malik's cell phone rings. It is his dad.

Malik: Hey, Dad.

Doctor: Hey, son, I want all the family to come over soon for dinner. I want you to bring Malena and the girls.

Malik: What's the occasion?

Doctor: I just want all my family to come together especially now. I'm still shaken about what could have happened to your sister.

Malik: Yes, I know. She told me about that. The station was blowing up with phone calls when it happened, but I didn't realize it was Ivy's plane until she called me.

Doctor: So will you bring the family and come?

Malik: We will be there, just let me know when.

Doctor: Okay, I will. I'll talk to you later, son. Love you.

Malik just hung up. He never was the mushy type to say I love you back.

Clay's Apartment

Mason: Answer me, Clay! Who were you talking to? Telling them you love them.

Clay froze up. He had to think of something quick, or Mason would catch on. Mason couldn't know he was talking to Mystery. Clay made himself cry.

Clay: That was my dad, Mason. He called to tell me a family friend had passed.

Mason felt little after Clay told him that.

Mason: Oh, I'm sorry about that, and I'm sorry for acting like a jerk. I thought something was going on.

Mason hugged Clay to comfort him. Even though Clay was lying, he had to play along to keep Mason from blowing up.

Clay: The funeral service is tomorrow. I need to go buy something to wear.

Mason: You want me to come with you?

Clay: No, it's okay. I am going to go by the hospital to see my dad first. He didn't sound right on the phone.

Mason: Okay, well, call me and let me know if everything is okay.

Clay: Okay, I will.

Clay got his keys and left.

Mystery's Place

Brazil: Mystery, are you ok with Mom staying here?

Mystery: Look, I will never forget what she did. I forgave her because I promised my mom before she died that I would. She's only staying until all this is over. That's it.

Brazil: I mean okay. That's your decision. Well, we need to be going. We just wanted to stop by and pay our respects.

Mystery: Thanks for coming by.

Ivy: Mystery, it was good to finally get to meet you.

Mystery: Likewise. So I will see you both tomorrow?

Brazil: Yep, we will be there.

Brazil, Ivan, and Ivy left.

At the Hospital

The doctor was in his office when there was a knock at the door.
Doctor: Come in.
Diane: Dr. Baker?
The doctor stood up and greeted Diane.
Doctor: Diane, come in. Have a seat. How are you?
Diane: I'm making it.
Doctor: How can I help you?
Diane: Well, I wanted to thank you for all you did for my sister. Mystery and I really appreciate it.
Doctor: No problem at all. That's my job. Gloria was a good lady.
They just stared at each other.
Diane: Oh, the service is going to be tomorrow at two. I hope you will be able to come.
Doctor: Unfortunately, I can't. I have to work a double tomorrow. I will definitely send some flowers. I hate I'm going to miss it. She is going to be missed.
Diane: Yes, she is.
Doctor: I hope I'm not going to overstep for what I'm about to say. Would you like to come by the hospital tomorrow after the service and have dinner with me?
Diane was shocked, but flattered. She felt the spark between them as well.
Doctor: I hope I didn't offend you.
Diane: Oh no, no, you didn't offend me. I would love to come by tomorrow and have dinner with you.
The doctor was glad she accepted.
Doctor: I hope you like hospital cafeteria food since I can't leave.
They both laughed.
Diane: That will be okay.
Diane stood up.
Diane: I got to go. I want to say thank you again.
Doctor: I'm glad you stop by. So I will see you tomorrow?
Diane: I will be here.
Diane left.

At the Hotel

Adriana: I can't believe that SOB is here in Atlanta.

Max: I know. I wonder how he found her.

Adriana: I don't know, but I am not leaving here until I feel like she is safe and okay.

Max: I'm right here with you.

Adriana: It's been a long day. I need to take a shower and relax. Want to join me?

Max: Sure, babe, I will be right there.

Adriana went to the bathroom. Max took out his cell and made a call. Call went straight to voice mail.

Max: Hey, it's Max. I'm in town, and I need to see you. Give me a call.

On the next episode, Gloria's funeral service takes place.

EPISODE 6

The home going service for Gloria was beautiful. The preacher gave an exceptional eulogy. The choir sounded wonderful. Mystery and Diane put her away nice. After the burial, everyone headed back to Mystery's house. The kitchen was full of food, and the living room was filled with flowers.

Mystery was exhausted and wanted to go lay down. He found Diane.

Mystery: Hey, can you handle and watch everything for a little bit? I want to go lay down. I'm drained.

Diane: Yes, of course. Are you okay?

Mystery: Yes, just want to be alone and lay down for a few minutes. I will be back down.

Diane: Okay.

Mystery was heading for the stairs when he ran into Ivy.

Ivy: Hey, Mystery, it was a beautiful services.

Mystery: Thank you. If you would excuse me, I'm going to go lay down for a minute.

Mystery walked upstairs. Brazil walked up.

Brazil: Everything okay?

Ivy: Oh yeah. Mystery said he needed to lay down for a minute. How are you doing?

Brazil: I'm okay. I mean I really didn't know her. I think we being here let Mystery know he is not alone. He still has a family.

Ivy: That's sweet of you. Now I remembered why I married you before.

They both laughed.

Ivy: I'm going to go get something drink and go check on Ivan. He's still outside with the other kids.

Brazil: Okay.

Malik's House

Malena was in the kitchen cooking when there was a knock at the door. She yelled out, "Just a minute." She washed and dried her hands, then went to answer the door. As soon as she opened it, she was surprised.

Malena: Armon?

Armon: How is my baby sister?

They hugged each other.

Malena: You're just getting in town?

Armon: I got here yesterday. Let me look at you. You're still beautiful just like Mom. Where are my nieces?

Malena called out, "Melanie? Ashley? Come down here for a minute.

They both came downstairs. When they saw their uncle, they ran to hug him.

Armon: You guys have gotten so big. You're not babies anymore, especially you, Melanie.

Melanie: Are you going to stay with us, Uncle Armon?

Armon: Oh no. I'm staying at a hotel downtown.

Ashley: You going to stay for dinner though, right?

Armon: That's up to your mom.

Malena: Of course you are. It's been too long. Girls, go finish cleaning up and let me talk to your uncle for a bit.

Melanie: I'm so glad you're here, Uncle Armon.

Ashley: Me too.
Armon: Me three.
They gave him a hug and went back upstairs.
Malena: So, Armon, what brings you to Atlanta?
Armon: I've found Alexandria and my son.

Mystery's Place

Clay was unable to get to Mystery the whole time. He saw him standing by the stairs and decided to go talk to him.

Clay: Hey, you, how are you doing?
Brazil (confused): I'm okay, thanks for asking.
Clay: Like I was telling you yesterday, I'm here for you, if you need me. I still love you.
Brazil: Excuse me. You don't even know me.
Clay: Mystery, why are you talking to me like this?
Brazil: Oooooh! Oh, you don't know.
Clay: Know what?
Brazil: I'm not Mystery. I'm Brazil, Mystery's twin.
Clay: Why are you messing with me?
Brazil: I'm not.
Ivy came back from getting her drink.
Ivy: Clay?
Clay: Hey, Ivy, I didn't see you at the church.
Ivy: Yeah, I didn't see you either. I see you met Brazil.
Clay: Wait a minute. This is the Brazil? Your ex-husband and Ivan's dad?
Ivy: Yes, I told you about him.
Clay: Oh my god, I'm so embarrassed right now. Please forgive me. I thought you were Mystery. It's nice to finally meet you. I'm Clay, Ivy's brother.
Brazil: No problem, and it's good to meet you too.
Clay: He never told me he had a twin.
Ivy: Wait a minute. I didn't put two and two together either. Mystery is your Mystery? The one you were in a relationship with?
Clay: Yep, that's the one.
They all laughed.

Clay: Sorry about that Brazil. Do you know where he is?
Brazil: He is upstairs.
Clay: Okay, I'm going to go say goodbye before I leave.
Clay went upstairs and knocked on Mystery's door.
Mystery: Come in.
Clay: Hey, it's me. Can I come in?
Mystery: Hey, you, come on in.
Clay: Were you sleeping?
Mystery: Naw, just lying here, thinking about my mom.
Mystery got up and sat on the side of the bed.
Mystery: You can come sit down.
Clay: Mystery, we need to talk.

On the next episode, Mystery and Clay have a heart to heart.

EPISODE 7

Malena: You've found them? Are you serious? Where?

Armon: They were here in Atlanta.

Malena: Here?

Armon: Yep. That's why I'm here.

Malena: How did you find them?

Armon: Private investigator. He was my last hope. I thought I had lost them forever.

Malena: Well, I'm glad you've found them. What are you going to do now?

Armon: I don't know. What I do know is she will not be taking my son away from me anymore, I bet you that.

Malena: Armon, you know I never liked when you talk like that.

Armon: Oh no, everything is going to fine. You need not worry about your big brother. I have everything under control now. So when can we eat? I'm starving, and it smells so good.

Malena: Now actually. Malik will not be home until in the morning. Melanie? Ashley? Come eat.

They came downstairs, and they all had a nice dinner.

Armon left afterward.

At the Hotel

Adriana: I can't believe Armon found Alexandria. He gives me the creeps. Always have.

Max: Come on now, baby, don't get yourself all worked up again.

Adriana: I know.

Max kissed her. His cell phone vibrated. He saw it was a text saying, "Meet me downtown by the Ferris wheel."

Adriana: Who was it?

Max: Oh, just some random text, trying to promote something.

Adriana: Oh, okay. I think I'm going to go over to Alexandria. Make sure she is okay. You want to come?

Max: No, you go ahead. I will stay here and unpack a little. Get everything in drawers and stuff. Tell Alexandria I asked about her.

Adriana said okay, gave him a kiss, then left. Max waited for about fifteen minutes, then left himself.

Mystery's Place

Mystery: What do you want to talk about?

Clay: Why you didn't tell me you had a twin brother?

Mystery: I actually just found out myself not too long ago.

Clay: So Gloria is not your mother? Who is?

Mystery: The lady you saw sitting next to me at the funeral. It's a long story.

Clay: Well, I'm here for you.

Mystery: I know you are.

Clay: No, Mystery, you don't get it.

Clay stood up.

Clay: I love you, Mystery. I'm still in love with you.

Mystery stood up and let out a deep breath.

Mystery: I love you too.

Clay was surprised to hear that.

Clay: You what?

Mystery put both hands on Clay's face.

Mystery: I said I love you too. I never stopped loving you.

Mystery gave Clay a long passionate kiss.

Clay: Wow, I thought I would never hear you say those words to me again.

Mystery: I know. You just hurt me so bad with what you did. I just couldn't let that go and come back to you like it never happened. The next thing I knew, you were actually with Mason and in a relationship.

Clay: I regret hurting you, and I regret turning to Mason. That was the worst mistake of my life. We can make it right now, if you want to.

Mystery: I'm going to be honest with you, Clay. I don't have a problem with that, but I am not going to be in a love triangle with you and Mason.

Clay: I don't expect you to.

Mystery: Clay, if you want to be with me and work on us, you have to leave Mason. You have to tell him you don't want him anymore and make him believe it.

Clay: I will try my best.

Mystery: Take your time. It's no rush. I'm not going anywhere. Now I have a question for you, and I need the honest truth if we are going to work on us.

Clay: Okay, ask me anything.

Mystery: What happened to your eye?

Clay lowered his head.

Clay: Mason hit me. It's better now though. It doesn't hurt, just ready for the blackness to go away.

Mystery lifted Clay's head up by his chin.

Mystery: You never had to worry about that when you were with me. You're too good for that, and you know it.

Clay: I know.

Mystery hugged Clay. They started kissing again. Diane walked in.

Diane (surprised): Oh, I'm sorry. I should have knocked.

Mystery: That's okay. Diane, this is Clay, my ex-boyfriend. Clay, this is Diane, my mother.

Diane was happy to hear Mystery introduce her as his mother.

Diane: Nice to meet you, Clay.

Clay: Nice to meet you too. I need to be getting home, so I will call you tomorrow and check on you.

Mystery: Okay.
Clay left.
Diane: I didn't mean to barge in. How long you two were together?
Mystery: A year. Was there something you needed?
Diane: Oh, just to tell you everyone had left and that I was leaving.
Mystery: Where are you going? I thought you were staying here.
Diane: I am. I'm going to go meet someone for dinner. I cleaned up everything downstairs, so you don't have to worry about that.
Mystery: I appreciate that. I appreciate everything you've done since Mom gone.
Diane: No problem, baby. Now I got to go.
Diane kissed Mystery on the cheek and left.

Downtown by the Ferris Wheel

Max walked up.
Max: Hey, I'm glad you came.
Malena: It's good to see you again, Max. How are you?
They hugged each other.

On the next episode, Diane and Dr. Baker have dinner. A secret is revealed.

EPISODE 8

Max: I'm well. You look nice.

Malena: Thank you. It's been a long time.

Max: I know, ten years.

Malena: What brings you back to Atlanta after all these years?

Max: I'm here with my wife. We're here visiting her sister.

Malena: Oh, okay. How is your wife? Are you both still teaching?

Max: She is good, and yes, we are. What about you and your husband?

Malena: He is good as well. He is still a police officer. As for me, I am just a stay-at-home mom.

Max: Oh, you gave up teaching?

Malena: Yes, after my last child, I decided to stay at home and be there more for them since their dad was always working.

Max: Are you sure that's the real reason?

At the Hospital

Diane went to the hospital for her dinner date with Dr. Baker. She knocked on his office door.

Doctor: Come in.

Diane: Hey, am I interrupting?

Doctor: Oh, no, of course not. I was actually just filing some papers away. I'm glad you came.

Diane: Me too.

Doctor: Shall we go to the cafeteria?

Diane: Sure.

They both headed to the cafeteria.

Alexandria's Place

Adriana had made it over to Alexandria's house. Alexandria was outside getting some air when she walked up.

Adriana: Hey, sis, is everything okay?

Alexandria: Yes, I just needed some fresh air. Do you see that black SUV there?

Adriana: Yes, what about it?

Alexandria: All the time I have stayed here, I have never seen that truck. I really think Armon has someone watching me.

Adriana: Are you sure? Let's go back inside.

They walked back in the apartment.

Adriana: Where are Jase and Armon?

Alexandria: Jase is in the room sleeping. Armon left last night but said he will be back.

Adriana: We should leave while he is gone. Come on, I will help you pack.

Alexandria: Adriana, I can't keep running from him. It's not fair to Jase or me. Anyway, he would just find me again.

Adriana: Speaking of, do you know how he did that? You were so careful.

Alexandria: I know, and I don't know how he found me. All I know is I can't keep running. I've made Atlanta my home, and I am staying here.

Adriana: Well, Max and I are not going anywhere any time soon, so if you need us, we are here.

Adriana hugged her sister.

Alexandria: Where is Max, by the way?

At the Hospital

Diane: Thanks for paying for my dinner. It was good.

Doctor: No problem, thank you for coming. I want to say I'm sorry again that I had to miss the funeral. I'm sure it was a nice service.

Diane: It was. Thank you for the flowers. They were beautiful.

Dr. Baker (gazing at Diane): Just like you.

As soon as he said that, he snapped out of his trance.

Doctor: Oh, I'm sorry.

Diane (smiling): Don't be sorry. I haven't had anyone tell me that in a while.

Doctor: Well, you are. So tell me something about yourself. If you are anything like Gloria, then I know you are a good woman.

Diane: I wouldn't go that far.

Doctor: Why you say that?

Diane: There's a lot of things I have done in my life growing up that I'm not proud of.

Dr. Baker (grabbing Diane's hand): Diane, me too. I wasn't always the good doctor, trust me. Everyone has a past. We should never let the past control or dictate our future."

Diane: You are right.

Doctor: Look, I will go first. I have three children and three grandchildren who are the love of my life. My wife died about five years ago.

Diane: Oh, I'm sorry to hear that. What happened?

Doctor: She had cancer. Now it's your turn.

Diane: I have twin boys and one grandchild. I've been married and divorced twice.

Doctor: Third time's the charm.

They both smiled at each other.

Downtown by the Ferris Wheel

Malena: What do you mean? Of course that is the reason.

Max held his hands up.

Max: I'm sorry. I wasn't trying to offend you. Let's walk to the park.

As they were heading to the park, Armon was walking back to his hotel and spotted them.

Armon: Now what is this about?

He decided to follow them. He followed them to the park and stood behind a tree where he could overhear what they were talking about.

Max: So how is she?

Malena: She is fine.

Max: Thank you for keeping me updated on everything throughout the years. You know this is hard for me.

Malena: I know. It's been hard for me too, but we made a promise, remember?

Max: We should have just come clean back then.

Malena: Max, I was married, and you were getting married that next week. Everything worked out the way it should have. No one needed to know the truth, especially now. Malik can never find out that we had an affair and that you are Ashley's real father.

Armon (to himself): Well, I'll be damned.

On the next episode, Armon confronts Max.

EPISODE 9

Armon could not believe what he had just heard.

Armon: Ashley is Max's child.

He continued to listen to Max and Malena's conversation.

Max: Malena, I know your husband can never find out. Neither can my wife. Even though it was a mistake that happened, we created something beautiful together, Ashley.

Malena: I know.

Max: I'm not asking for you to tell her the truth. All I want is to see her. Can you make that happen?

Malena: I will see what I can do. I got to go.

Max: Malena, please do this for me.

Malena: Good night, Max. I will be in touch.

Malena left. Max stood there for a moment, then left. Armon followed him.

Alexandria's Place

Alexandria: Where is Max, by the way?

Adriana: He stayed at the hotel to finish unpacking. He is worried about this situation. We both are.

Alexandria: I know, but I will be okay. I told Armon there is no getting back together at all.

Adriana: I don't trust him.

Alexandra: Me either. Trust me. My eyes are wide open when it comes to him.

Adriana: I should hope so. Well, I'm going to get back to the hotel. If you need us, do not hesitate to call.

Alexandria: I won't.

They hugged each other, and Adriana left.

At the Hospital

Doctor: So you have twins, huh? Do they live here in Atlanta?

Diane: As a matter of fact, they do. You have met one of them already.

Doctor: Really who? When?

Diane: Mystery.

Doctor: Mystery is your son? I thought—

Diane (interrupted): It's a long story. Long story short, Gloria raised Mystery as her own. Remember when I told you I have done some things that I wasn't proud of?

Doctor: Oh, I'm not judging at all.

Diane: Needless to say, Mystery just found out himself, and he is adjusting to it. I'm just trying to be here now for him as he needs me.

Doctor: I understand that.

Diane: Well, it's getting late. I better let you get back to your work.

Doctor: Yeah, I have another round to make, then I will be leaving myself. I would love to see you again.

Diane: I would like that. Here is my number.

Diane wrote her number on a napkin and gave it to him.

Diane: Call me sometime.

Doctor: I sure will.

Diane stood up and gave him a kiss on the cheek, then left.

At the Hotel

Max had made it back to his room. He wasn't in there a minute, when there was a knock at the door. He thought maybe Adriana had left her key. When he opened the door, he was surprised to see Armon.

Max: What the hell are you doing here?
Armon: Can I talk to you for a second?
Max: We have nothing to talk about. How did you know what hotel we were in, better yet what room number?
Armon: Can you just give me five minutes, then I will leave.
Max did not invite him in. He stepped outside to talk to him.
Max: What is it?
Armon: I need your help. I know Adriana had to tell Jase something about me for him to treat me the way he did. After you both left, he wouldn't talk to me at all. I know what I did to Alexandria was wrong, but that didn't give her the right to disappear with my son for almost a year. Will you please talk to him for me? Convince him to at least talk to me.
Max started laughing.
Armon: What's funny?
Max: It wasn't Adriana who told Jase the horrible thing you did to his mother. It was me. You don't deserve to be around him, either of them for what you did. When Alexandria showed up at our house, she was a wreck. You did that. What kind of man puts his wife in the hospital?
Armon: So it was you. You took it upon yourself to brainwash my kid against me. Who gave you that right? I was hoping to have a civilize conversation with you, but I see that's out the window now.
Armon got in Max's face.
Armon: You will help me. As a matter of fact, you will tell Jase you lied to him about me. That you made a mistake and to give me a chance.
Max: What make you think I will do anything to help you?
Armon smirked arrogantly.
Armon: Because if you don't, I will tell Adriana about your daughter Ashley.

On the next episode, Armon blackmails Max.

EPISODE 10

Max: What did you say?

Armon: You heard me. If you don't talk to Jase and tell him you made a mistake about me, I will tell Adriana you have a daughter. Ashley, is it?

Max was totally stunned by what he was hearing.

Max: You don't know what you're talking about. I don't have a daughter.

Armon laughed.

Armon: You don't have to lie. I followed you tonight. You met this woman at the park downtown. I wonder what Adriana would think if she finds out her perfect hubby cheated a week before their wedding and had a baby.

Max was speechless.

Armon: I thought that would catch your attention.

Max: So you're going to blackmail me into helping you? Is that it?

Armon: Call it what you want.

Max: You can't tell Adriana. That would devastate her.

Armon: Then, I guess I have my answer.

Max: How do I know you won't tell her anyway?

Armon: You don't. That's the price you pay for sticking your nose in my business.

Max: Adriana can't find out.

Adriana walked up and was surprised.

Adriana: Can't find out what?

Alexandria's Place

Alexandria was sitting in the living room watching television. Jase was already out for the night sleeping in her bed. There was a knock at the door. Alexandria went to answer. It was Brazil. She hadn't seen him in almost a week. She was glad he stopped by. When she opened the door, she ran into his arms.

Brazil: I take it you miss me.

Alexandria: Shut up, you know I do. You don't miss me?

Brazil: Of course, that's why I stopped by.

They both sat on the sofa side by side.

Alexandria: There has been so much going on lately you wouldn't believe.

Brazil: Oh, I can believe it. I'm sorry I didn't reach out to you sooner. Did you see on the news about the plane crash last week?

Alexandria nodded yes.

Brazil: My son and ex-wife was on that plane, but they got off to take a later flight.

Alexandria just covered her mouth with her hand.

Brazil: I was a complete mess before I found out they were alive. Then on top of that, Gloria, Mystery's mom, died. They buried her today.

Alexandria: Oh my god, I didn't know. I will go see him tomorrow. I'm so glad your son and ex-wife got off that plane. Sorry I couldn't have been there for you.

Brazil: It's okay. You didn't know. What's been going on with you?

Alexandria: Well, you remember the story I told you on why I moved to Atlanta?

Brazil: Yeah, you wanted to get away from your husband because of what he did to you.

Alexandria: Yes, well, he found me. He showed up at my door a few days ago and threatened me and made all these demands.

Brazil couldn't say a word. It was because of him that her husband had found her anyway.

Brazil: What do mean he threatened you?

Alexandria: He actually pulled a gun out on me and said he would kill me if I called the police. He said he has someone watching and following me. Do you know how that feels to have someone out there constantly watching you and you have no idea who it is?

Brazil now felt he was the blame. He didn't think her husband would actually come here and threaten to kill her. He should have believed Alexandria completely and turned down the job to find her.

Brazil: Where is he now?

Alexandria: He is here in Atlanta. He is not going anywhere.

Brazil: I'm sorry to hear all this. You don't plan on leaving again, are you?

Alexandria: No, I am done running. I have made a life here now. I don't want to start all over again and put my son through that. I'm just going to stay here and let Armon see Jase when he wants, but he knows there is no getting back together for us.

Brazil: I feel somewhat responsible.

Alexandria: What do you mean? Why would you be responsible.

Clay's Apartment

Clay was in the kitchen, cooking fried chicken and rice when Mason came in. Clay could tell Mason had an attitude about something because he didn't say one word when he came in. He went and got a beer out the fridge and slammed the door. Clay jumped.

Mason: Clay, the funeral you went to. Who was it?

Clay could feel an argument coming.

Clay: Why you ask?

Mason: Just answer the damn question. I just want to see if you're going to tell me the truth.

Clay: Her name was Gloria. We all went to the same church.

Mason: We all as in you, your family, Gloria, and Mystery? Gloria is Mystery's mom, right?

Clay (nervous): Yeah.

Mason: Why didn't you tell me that when I first asked you, instead of saying a family friend? Did you not think I would find out? You do remember Mystery, Malik, and I were all best friends and stayed at each other's house, right?

Clay: I didn't think it was a big deal.

Mason walked up next to Clay while he was flipping the chicken.

Mason: Oh, so you getting smart with me now? I will throw this chicken grease in your face.

Mason took a drink of the beer and sprayed it out of mouth on Clay. Clay just stood there saying nothing.

Mason: Did you talk to Mystery?

Clay wiped his face.

Clay: No, he was with his family. After the service, I left and came back here. I didn't even go back to the house.

Clay knew he was lying, but he needed to smooth over this conversation before it got worst. Clay was done cooking.

Clay: The food is ready.

Clay went to the bathroom and cleaned himself up and got ready for bed, leaving Mason up.

Lying in bed, all Clay could think about was what Mystery told him. The only way he could be with him was to leave Mason.

Clay (to himself): I will tell Mason tomorrow that it's over.

On the next episode, Alexandria and Brazil gets close.

EPISODE 11

Adriana: Max, what can't I find out, baby, and why in the hell is he here?

Max was shocked to see Adriana.

Max: Babe, I didn't see you come up.

Adriana: Obviously, but you didn't answer me. What can't I find out?

Max and Armon both looked at each other, Armon with a smirk on his face.

Max: Baby, I didn't want you to find out that he was here. I knew it would upset you.

Adriana: Why are you here, Armon?

Armon: I just come to clear the air.

Adriana: Clear the air about what? We already know what happened and what you did. You put my sister in the hospital, so she ran for her life.

Armon: Adriana, I regret that. I do. You know I love your sister.

Adriana laughed.

Adriana: That is really funny.

Armon: Look, I know you don't like me now more than ever, but that doesn't change the fact that Alexandria and I have a son together. She didn't have the right to just take him and run away for almost a year.

Adriana: Are you serious? What was she supposed to do then, just stay there and wait for you to put her in the hospital again? As far as I'm concerned, she had every right.

Armon: Okay, I'm not getting anywhere with you I see. I'm just going to leave.

Adriana: Yes, you do just that and don't come back here again.

Armon: You both have a nice night.

Looking dead at Max, Armon said, "I will be in touch." Then he left.

Adriana and Max went into the room.

Adriana: What did he mean by that?

Max: Mean by what?

Adriana: That he will be in touch.

Max: I don't know. He probably just said that to get under our skin. Who knows what goes on in his mind? How is your sister?

Adriana: She's okay. She said she is done running. She is just going to deal with Armon and let him be in Jase's life. I can't pretty much blame her. We just need to make sure she is okay before we leave here.

Max: I'm with you, babe.

Max could only think about the threat that Armon made. He will tell Adriana everything if he didn't help him.

Adriana: Baby, let's go to bed.

Max: Sure.

They turned in for the night.

Alexandria's Place

Alexandria: It's not your fault. Why would you be responsible?

Brazil: I should have been here when he showed up.

Alexandria: There would not have been anything you could have done. Anyway, my sister and brother-in-law were here.

Brazil: Oh, they're here from Florida?

Alexandria: Yes, they brought my son to me.

Brazil: Oh, your son is here too?

Alexandria: Yes, he is back there in my room, asleep for the night. My sister and brother-in-law got a hotel room.

Brazil: I'm glad you have your son back in spite of the circumstances. Maybe it's for the best that Armon is here. He can see that you are happy and have moved on.

Alexandria: No, Armon being here is not for the best. I wish he had never found me. I only wish I knew how he did it because I was so careful. The only people that knew where I was were my sister and brother-in-law, and they definitely didn't tell him. Then, there were you and Mystery, but Armon don't even know you two. I just don't know how he did it. Guess he is more resourceful than I thought.

Brazil (feeling guilty): Let's just change the subject. I've missed you.

Alexandria (smiling): Oh, you do? Well, show me how much.

Brazil leaned over and kissed her on the lips. He stopped, and they both stared in each other eyes. They both started kissing each other again very passionately trading each other tongues. Brazil kissed her on the side of her face and slowly down to her neck. Alexandria's eyes went to the back of her head. It's been so long since she had someone to make her feel so good. She grabbed on to him as she reached down and pulled off his shirt. He returned the favor by pulling off hers as well. They both stared at each other again for a second. Alexandria reached behind her back and unsnapped her bra, sliding it off slowly. Brazil began to become very aroused and erect. He started kissing her on the neck again, then very slowly inch his way down to her chest. He grabbed both of her breasts as he continued to kiss and lick her stomach. He then put one of her breast in his mouth. The heat from his mouth made her very hot. She grabbed on to him tighter. Brazil then stood up and took off his pants and boxers. Alexandria, very happy with what she was seeing, took off her shorts and panties as well. She stood up. Brazil leaned and kissed her. He then picked her up. She wrapped her legs around his waist and slid down on him slowly, they both still kissing one another. He carried her to the guest bedroom and closed the door behind them. There they made love all night.

On the next episode, Diane thinks about her past.

EPISODE 12

Diane was up watching television when her phone rang. She saw it was Dr. Baker and got excited.

Diane: Hello.

Doctor: Good morning, and how are you?

Diane: I'm good, and you?

Doctor: I'm fine. I was just thinking about you. Would you like to have brunch with me this morning? I don't have to be to the hospital until later this evening.

Diane: Sure. Where do you want me to meet you?

Doctor: Oh no, I will come pick you up. You're at Gloria's, right?

Diane: Yes.

Doctor: I am only five minutes away from there.

Diane: Okay, I will be ready when you get here.

Diane got up and slipped on something more casual. Dr. Baker was right about being five minutes away. There was a knock at the door. Mystery came out of his room to go answer, but Diane was already downstairs. She opened the door.

Diane: Hey you.

They both smiled at each other.

Doctor: Hey yourself. Sorry for the short notice but are you ready. Diane smiling said, "That's ok and I am."

Coming downstairs Mystery said, "Are you going somewhere?"

Diane: Yes, I'm going to go have brunch with Dr. Baker. You remember him, right.

Mystery: Of course I do. Nice to meet you again, Doctor.

Doctor: Likewise.

They both shook hands.

Doctor: I'm sorry again about Gloria.

Mystery: Thanks. Well, don't let me keep you guys. Have fun.

Diane gave Mystery a kiss on the cheek, then she and Dr. Baker left.

Clay's Apartment

Mason had fell asleep on the sofa last night while Clay was in the bedroom. Clay was up in the bathroom, getting dressed. Mason was still asleep on the sofa when he was awakened by music coming from the kitchen. He got up to check it out. He saw it was Clay's cell phone. He saw that Clay had a missed call. When he checked the call, it was a missed call from Mystery. All of a sudden, a text from Mystery came through while Mason was checking the phone. The text read, "Thinking about you. I'm not rushing you, but I was wondering when you plan on telling Mason the truth. That's the only way we can be together again, if you tell him it's over. By the way, it was good to hold you in my arms again. Talk to you later."

Mason was livid.

Downtown Café

Diane and the doctor had finished their brunch. They were just sipping on their coffee, talking at this point.

Diane: Thank you for the meal, Dr. Baker.

Doctor: Please call me Joshua, and you are very welcome. I'm going to be honest. I like you a lot, Diane. I really would like us to get to know each other more and become closer.

Diane: Why thank you. I really would like that too.

Dr. Baker grabbed her hand and kissed it. All of a sudden, a guy walked up to his table.

Kennedy: Jo Jo, what's up, man?

Doctor: Ken Ken, what's going on?

They both shook hands and gave each other a hug.

Kennedy: Who is the beautiful lady here?

Doctor: Kennedy, this is Diane. Diane, meet Kennedy, one of my best friends and frat brothers.

Kennedy shook her hand.

Kennedy: Nice to meet you, Diane. Now tell me why is such a beautiful woman hanging out with a dope like this?

Dr. Baker punched him on the arm.

Doctor: Hey, hey now.

They all laughed.

Kennedy: We still on for going fishing next week, right?

Doctor: Oh sure, no doubt. Make sure you remind Jackson. You know how forgetful he is.

Kennedy: I will call him. Well, I don't want to keep you from this lovely lady here. It was nice to meet you, Diane. I will call you later, Jo Jo.

Doctor: Okay.

Kennedy left. Dr. Baker sat down.

Diane: Jo Jo?

Doctor: You heard that, huh?

Diane: Yes, I did, Dr. Joshua Baker. Tell me the story behind that nickname because I swear, I have heard that nickname somewhere before. Ken Ken as well.

The doctor laughed.

Doctor: Well, me, Kennedy, and Jackson all met in college. We were in the same fraternity and became the best of friends. We gave each other those nicknames back then. They called me Jo Jo, short for Joshua. We called Kennedy Ken Ken and called Jackson JJ because he had two last names for a name, Jackson Jones. When we became older and established, we went back to addressing ourselves with our real names. We only called each other by our nicknames when we are hanging out.

Diane: So you all stay in touch with one another.

Doctor: Oh sure. We all stay here in Atlanta and very close with each other families. Kennedy is the chief of police here. My oldest son, Malik, works for him. He has a wife and two kids. His daughter, Sarah, works at a law office in Alpharetta where she lives. His son, Caleb, is in prison.

Diane: I'm sorry to hear that. What did he do, if I may ask?

Doctor: Oh, don't be sorry. Kennedy loves his kids but is very open about his family. Caleb raped his ex-girlfriend. He was sentenced to five years for it. He should be getting out next month though. Kennedy just could not get a grip on Caleb. He did all he could to raise him right, he and his wife. He just was a rebellious child.

Diane: What about your other friend?

Doctor: Jackson? Jackson was the wildest one of us all. He owns two bars here downtown. He is more of a loner. He never wanted to be married and definitely didn't want kids. He liked having his freedom and different women. Even today, he doesn't want a wife or any kids, but he loves Kennedy and my kids to death, go figure.

Diane: I can't imagine not wanting kids at all, but to each his own, I guess. I know this sounds weird, but I have heard those nicknames somewhere before, seems like. This is going to bother for a minute.

They both laughed.

Doctor: I guess I better be taking you back. I need to get over to the hospital.

They both left.

Clay's Apartment

Clay came from the bedroom, looking around. He went to the kitchen looking around as well. Mason was up sitting in the recliner.

Mason: Looking for this?

Clay was surprised to see Mason with his cell phone.

Clay: Yes, I thought I had lost it.

Clay went to go get it from Mason.

Mason: It woke me up this morning. Someone was calling you. So I checked it.

Clay: You checked my phone?

Mason stood up.

Mason: I did. Here you go, check your last missed call and tell me who it was.

Mason gave the cell phone to Clay.

Mason: Oh, and check you last text message and tell me what it says.

Clay hands started shaking as he was going through his phone. He saw where Mystery had called him and text him. He read the text to himself. Clay slowly lifted his head and looked at Mason.

Mason punched him in the face, knocking him to the floor.

Mystery's Place

The doctor had dropped Diane off. She was so exhausted for some reason. Mystery was upstairs in his room. Diane laid on the sofa to take a nap. She started dreaming.

Diane was standing on the corner of New York twenty-six years ago. She had on a low-cut shirt and a very short mini skirt with some black thigh boots on. There were five other girls on that same corner. She had already made $500, and the night was still young. A car pulled up.

Driver: What's up, hottie?

Diane: What's up with you?

Driver: Me and my boys looking for some fun. Can you help with that?

Diane: Sure can, baby, if the money is right. What are you offering?

Driver: We got it all: liquor, weed, ecstasy, coke, and we will put $600 in your panties.

Diane: Well, let's go.

Diane got in the back of the car, and they headed to a motel.

Driver: So what's your name?

Diane: I'm Trixie.

Passenger: I like that name. I bet you got some tricks for us tonight too.

Diane: Sure do. What's up with your boy back here?

Passenger: Oh, he's just high. He has been smoking all night. He probably won't be able to do much of nothing when we get to the room.

They all laughed.

Diane: What are your names?
Driver: I'm JJ. My man here is Ken Ken, and the sleepyhead in the back is Jo Jo.
Diane woke up in shock.
Diane: Oh my god, I remember. I know them.

On the season finale, an epic fight between Mystery and Mason.

EPISODE 13—
SEASON FINALE

Clay's Apartment

Mason punched Clay in the face, knocking him to the floor.

Mason (yelling): So you have been seeing him behind my back? Get the hell up, you weak bitch!

Clay slowly got up. He started to explain nervously.

Clay: I didn't want you to find out like this. I was going to talk to you today. Mason, I'm not happy with you, and I don't want to be in this relationship with you anymore.

Mason got in Clay's face.

Mason: So you're leaving me for him! Huh! Is that it?

Mason head-butted him. Out of nowhere and to his own surprise, Clay punched Mason in his face. He couldn't believe he did that.

Mason grabbed Clay by the neck, choking him. He punched him twice in the stomach, then his face. He threw Clay on the floor, kicking him in the side and stomach.

Mason: You're not going anywhere.

Mason then kicked Clay in the face. Clay was out cold. Blood oozed from his mouth and nose. Mason went to the bathroom to clean the sweat from his face. When he returned to the living room, Clay was gone.

Mystery's Place

Diane could not believe it. She knew Joshua and his friends. She needed to talk to him and fast, so she called him.

The doctor's phone rings.

Doctor: Hey, you.

Diane: Joshua, I need to talk to you.

Doctor: Okay, what is it?

Diane: No, not over the phone. I need to talk to you face-to-face.

Doctor: Okay, I'm about to do another round. If you leave now, you should be here by the time I finish. Just wait in my office.

Diane: Okay, I'm on my way.

Doctor: Diane, you sound upset so take your time.

Diane: I will.

They hung up, and Diane headed out the door.

Mystery heard the door closed, so he came downstairs. He saw that Diane had left. He went to the kitchen to get him something to drink and came back to the sofa to watch television. About thirty minutes later, there was a knock at the door. He went to answer it. As soon as he opened the door, Clay fell through. Mystery caught him.

Mystery: Clay? Clay, baby, what happened?

They fell to the floor. Mystery could see Clay was badly beaten. His face was swollen, his eye swollen shut, and dry blood all over his face from his nose and lips.

Clay (barely speaking): I did it. I told Mason. He said I was a weak bitch.

Clay fainted right there from exhaustion. Mystery just sat there on the floor, holding and rocking him.

Mystery: I'm so sorry. I'm so sorry.

He got up and carried Clay to the sofa. He went and got the first-aid kit and began doctoring on his face. Clay began to come to.

Mystery: Clay, I'm so sorry. This is all my fault.

Clay: No, it's not.

Wiping the blood off his face with a wet cloth, Mystery started to become angry.

Mystery: Where is Mason?

Clay: Home, I guess. I just left when I had the chance.

Mystery: I'm going over there.

Mystery started to get up, and Clay stopped him.

Clay: Please don't, Mystery. It will only make matters worse. Just let me lie here in your lap.

Clay laid there while Mystery continued to clean him up. Mystery was burning up inside. He saw that Clay finally had dosed off.

Mystery: Clay? Clay?

Mystery eased his head out of his lap and put a pillow under it. He looked at Clay's swollen face.

Mystery: This ends tonight.

Mystery left a note on the table saying, "I can't let this go." He got his keys and left.

Clay woke up ten minutes later. He didn't see Mystery. He sat up and saw the note on the table and read it.

Clay: No, Mystery, no.

He knew exactly where Mystery was going. He got his keys and ran out the house.

Malik's House

Malik was done getting ready for work. He headed downstairs and saw Malena was in the kitchen.

Malik: Hey, babe, I'm going to leave.

Malena: Okay, hon, be safe now.

Malik gave her a kiss and left out the house. Malena dialed Max.

Max: Hello.

Malena: Can you talk?

Max: Yes, of course. She went downstairs to the lobby.

Malena: I'm going to make arrangements so you can see your daughter.

Malik was about to get his car when Ivy pulled up. She got out.

Ivy: Hey, big bro. Are you leaving?

Malik: Yeah, I got to do a double tonight.

Ivy: Man, I was hoping to see you for a little while but duty calls. I understand that.

Malik: Yeah, it does. I will let you know the next time I'm off though. Malena is in there up though.

Ivy: Oh great, I can go talk to her then. Don't work too hard now.

Malik: I will try not to.

They gave each other hugs, and Malik left. Ivy headed on inside the house. She could hear Malena in the kitchen, but she was talking to somebody.

Max: Thank you for this, Malena. Maybe someday, Ashley and I can get to know each other.

Malena: Max, don't, okay. For that to happen, I will have to tell her the truth and Malik. I'm not going to do that. You need to understand that. I love my husband and don't want to lose him. If he finds out that he is not Ashley's father, he will leave me.

Ivy: What did you say?

Malena jumped dropping the phone to the floor.

Malena: Ivy.

Ivy: You just said Malik is not Ashley's father.

At the Hospital

Diane had made it to the hospital and was waiting in the doctor's office. She was pacing back and forth. The doctor finally walked in. All she could do was hug him.

Doctor: What's wrong?

Diane: You have to sit down for this.

The doctor sat down behind his desk. Diane started to explain.

Diane: Joshua, we have met before.

Doctor: I doubt that. You are from up north, and I haven't been there in years.

Diane: I know. Think about it for a minute. About twenty-six years ago, weren't you in New York?

Doctor: Oh my god, Diane, twenty-six years ago. I don't remember. I don't remember where I was a year ago.

He laughed.

Diane: Joshua, this is not a laughing matter. I need you to remember.

He saw how serious she was.

Diane: You and your friends, Kennedy and Jackson, were in New York for something. I don't know what it was, but that night, you all pick up a prostitute and took her to a motel.

Dr. Baker, looking confused, began to remember.

Doctor: What a minute. I think I do remember something like that. We all went to New York for our summer break and to catch a baseball game. We drank and got high all day. I remember Jackson was driving, and I was in the backseat. We did pick up a girl that night. I was really drunk and high that night. I remember going back to the room, smoking and passing out. I didn't even touch the girl that night. But wait a minute, how do you know about this, because I didn't tell you.

Diane: Joshua, that girl was me.

Dr. Baker laughed.

Doctor: Come on, stop playing. Did Kennedy get in contact with you and tell you?

Diane: No, it was me.

The doctor saw she was serious.

Doctor: Okay, if that was you, what was your name back then, because I do remember that, and it sure wasn't Diane?

Diane: My street name was Trixie.

The doctor knew then she was that girl.

Doctor: Oh, wow, okay. This is awkward now, and the reason I say that is because I know what took place that night. I mean, I still like you, Diane, and that was years ago. I hope this doesn't affect us.

Diane: It's just one problem.

Doctor: What is that?

Diane: That was the night I got pregnant with my twin boys, and either Kennedy or Jackson is their father.

Clay's Apartment

Mason was in the kitchen about to pop a beer when there was someone bamming at the door.

Mason: I'm coming, damn it!
More bamming came. Mason snatched the door open.
Mason: What!
It was Mystery.
Mystery walked past him.
Mystery: We need to talk.
Mason: You don't just barge in my house like you stay here.
Mystery was fuming.
Mystery: To hell with all that. We need to talk.
Mason: I don't have a damn thing to say to you.
Meanwhile, Clay was speeding, trying to make it home. He had run two red lights already and passing everyone that was in his way.
Clay (to himself): Please, Mystery, don't do anything crazy.
Mystery: I saw what you did to Clay's face.
Mason got in Mystery's face.
Mason: And so what? You're his savior now?
They just stood there, staring each other down.
Mystery: He said you like hitting weak bitches.
Mason: Some weak bitches like Clay deserve to be hit.
Boiling, Mystery took a deep breath.
Mystery: You know what? We have something in common.
Mason: Yeah, and what's that?
Mystery: I like hitting weak bitches too.
As soon as he said that, he punched Mason in the mouth. Mason grabbed his mouth. When he looked in his hand, he saw blood.
Mason: So this is what you've come to do, huh?
Mason went to the door and locked it.
Mason: Let's do this.

They both charged for each other. Tackling each other, Mystery punched Mason in the face twice. He went to throw another, but Mason blocked it and punched him in the face. Mason grabbed Mystery's neck, choking him. He pushed Mystery into a glass-framed portrait hanging on the wall while still choking him. The portrait shattered into pieces. Mystery tried to remove Mason's hand from around his neck but couldn't. Mason was only gripping tighter. Mystery then kneed Mason in the groins. No choice but to let Mystery go, Mason grabbed himself in pain. Mystery was coughing, trying to catch his breath. He then charged at Mason, and they both went over the living room table. Mystery got on top of him, punching him several times in his face. Mason picked up a glass ashtray on the floor that was knocked off the table. He hit Mystery on the side of the head with it. Mystery rolled off. They both staggered to stand up and catch their balance. Both covered and dripping with blood, they charge for each other again.

Clay finally pulled up to his apartment building and jumped out of the car, leaving it running. He ran up four flights of stairs. He could hear the rumbling before he got to his door. When he got to it, it was locked. He banged on the door, yelling for them to stop and open the door. That was not helping at all. All he could hear was rumbling and things breaking. He patted his pockets for the house key. He then realized that the house key was on his car key ring and that he had left the car running.

Clay: Shit.

He ran back down the stairs and cut the car off, snatching the keys out of the ignition. Clay ran back up four flights of stairs. He was out of breath. When he got to the door, he was so nervous that he dropped the keys.

Clay: Damn it! They are going to kill each other!

Mystery and Mason were still going at it like two raging bulls. Both were bloody and giving each other blows to the face and head. Mystery charged at Mason, and they went through the balcony glass doors. Clay finally unlocked the door and busted in. The apartment was a mess, like a tornado had been through it. He didn't care. He needed to stop them. He yelled out as he ran toward them. Not stopping, Mason punched Mystery in the stomach, Mystery grabbed him. Before Clay could reach them, they both fell up against the balcony wooden railing. The weight and force from them both was so great the railing broke, and they both went over falling four stories to the concrete parking lot.

To be continued.

ABOUT THE AUTHOR

Shawn Pierce was born and raised in Georgia. He is a graduate of Georgia Southern University with a B.A. degree in Accounting. Shawn has been employed with an engineering firm for the last six years. He owns his own trucking company called Pierce Trucking and currently lives in Atlanta, Georgia. Shawn always felt that he could be a great book/film writer for an audience, so he finally took the chance to explore the writing world with his first book, *Mystery*.

CPSIA information can be obtained at www.ICGtesting.com
Printed in the USA
LVOW04s0604110915

453755LV00001B/24/P